a novel in verse

KARMA

a novel in verse

Cathy Ostlere

PUFFIN
CANADA

PUFFIN CANADA

Published by the Penguin Group

Penguin Group (Canada), 90 Eglinton Avenue East, Suite 700, Toronto, Ontario, Canada M4P 2Y3
(a division of Pearson Canada Inc.)

Penguin Group (USA) Inc., 375 Hudson Street, New York, New York 10014, U.S.A.
Penguin Books Ltd, 80 Strand, London WC2R 0RL, England
Penguin Ireland, 25 St Stephen's Green, Dublin 2, Ireland (a division of Penguin Books Ltd)
Penguin Group (Australia), 250 Camberwell Road, Camberwell, Victoria 3124, Australia
(a division of Pearson Australia Group Pty Ltd)
Penguin Books India Pvt Ltd, 11 Community Centre, Panchsheel Park, New Delhi – 110 017, India
Penguin Group (NZ), 67 Apollo Drive, Rosedale, Auckland 0632, New Zealand
(a division of Pearson New Zealand Ltd)
Penguin Books (South Africa) (Pty) Ltd, 24 Sturdee Avenue, Rosebank,
Johannesburg 2196, South Africa

Penguin Books Ltd, Registered Offices: 80 Strand, London WC2R 0RL, England

Published in Puffin Canada hardcover by Penguin Group (Canada), a division of Pearson Canada Inc.,
2011. Simultaneously published by Razorbill, an imprint of Penguin Group (USA) Inc.

1 2 3 4 5 6 7 8 9 10

LIBRARY AND ARCHIVES CANADA CATALOGUING IN PUBLICATION

Ostlere, Cathy
Karma / Cathy Ostlere.

ISBN 978-0-670-06452-6

I. Title.

PS8629.S57K37 201   jC813'.6   C2010-907880-2

American Library of Congress Cataloging in Publication data available

Visit the Penguin Group (Canada) website at **www.penguin.ca**

Special and corporate bulk purchase rates available; please see
www.penguin.ca/corporatesales or call 1-800-810-3104, ext. 2477 or 2474

for John Pearce

If I die today, every drop of my blood
will invigorate the nation.

Indira Gandhi

Do not be deceived by the illusion
of the world, O Azad,
The whole realm of experience is but
a loop in the net of thy thought.

Azad, Urdu mystic poet

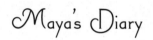

Maya's Diary

October 28, 1984

A brand-new diary

How to begin.
Click.
How. To. Begin.
Click. Click. Click.
I like the sound of a ballpoint pen.
Click. Click. Click. Click. Click.

I'll start with the date:
October 28, 1984.

Now the place:
Floating in air over ice.
Thirty-seven thousand feet, the pilot said.

But where exactly?
What latitude and longitude?
Is it Canada or Greenland
that fell away like a great sinking heart?
Is that a rising sun or a setting one?
The golden rays cut loose from India's plains.

Where am I really?
Nowhere, I guess.
Somewhere between an old life and a new.

Salutation

Every diary needs one.
A word of greeting to begin it all
the gentle endearment —
Dear

(My *D* bulges into the
margin like a soft balloon.)

Now, a name.
For the one who will listen.

Anne Frank used *Kitty*. The cat left behind, I
once believed. I was wrong. It was just a name. I
could use *Smoke*, my real cat left behind, but his
eyes are too pale. You can't confide to yellow
irises and patchy fur. Besides, the cat likes to
carry the dead in his mouth.

Just a month ago I might have used *Helen*. My
only friend. *Helen of Elsinore*, we used to joke. *The
face that launched a thousand tractors*. But even in the
country, the beautiful never understand the lonely.

I think of *Michael*.

(I can't stop myself.)

Backrow Michael, sitting behind me in homeroom.
Blue eyes. Blond hair. Perfect white
teeth gnawing on his lower lip. Angelic. I
imagine the entry:

Dear Michael,
I am flying and thinking of you. This is what I
remember: You took my braid and wrapped it
around your neck like a black satin ribbon. You
pulled my face to your cheek. You breathed on
me, whispering, Who are you? *When you bit*
my hair, I thought I'd die. Pleasure. Shame.
Your lips. On me.

But you can't address a boy in a diary, even if you
like him.

There's a black snake around my neck, Michael
shouted. *It's choking me!* Everyone in the hallway
looked. Laughed. Michael pretended to wrestle
with my braid until I slipped and fell. On top of
him. My sari unraveling like I was coming apart.

No, you can't address a boy, even if you think you
love him.

And especially, if he loves someone else.

Dear Diary

This remains the simple choice.
The anonymous confidante.
Clear and to the point.

But then what's the point of private words
lingering on the page, undirected? There must be
a listener. *The truest friend*, Anne had insisted.

Yes. A friend. And now I know.

I write the letter *M*.
Four strokes with the pen,
two peaks, a mountain of a letter.

The letter *a* follows —lowercase,
the necessary vowel.

And then I mean to write a *t*
and then a second *a* —
a perfectly balanced word for my longing:

    Mata

The name I call my mother.

But my hand slips or is it my mind? The pen dips
on the page, ink fading with the sudden upturned
sweep of a *y*. A second *a* appears:

Maya

The name that only my mother calls me.

The pen continues to move across the empty page.

Remember.
Remember that I love you.

host

Can the dead really speak?
Through the hand and pen of the living?

A mother's voice floats in from the edge of the
world. A daughter hears the whispers.

Or is it loneliness that conjures
the loved one from the ash?

No one wants to be forgotten.
Not the dead or the living.

I loved you too, Mata.
But why did you do what you did?

Northern lights

The pilot steers along ribbons of light. Green
polar flames rippling in the dark. Long silken
scarves floating on the air. It's like watching the
wind on fire. Pulsing.

Bapu sleeps beside me. His face is peaceful for
the first time in weeks. Perhaps he's dreaming this
aurora borealis into being—streams of wedding
garlands waving like underwater weeds. Guests
dancing.

My father's yellow turban rests on his knee.
A *closed lotus blossom*, my mother had once
described it, her hands tracing the folds, looking
for its beginning and its end.

I don't often see my father's hair uncovered.
Only on Saturday mornings when Mata washed
his belief in the bathroom sink. The long black river
flowing from his head. As long as his faith.

I caught glimpses of the tender ritual when I
passed down the hall. Bapu, in a chair,
leaning back against the white porcelain. My
mother's hands pouring water over the brow, the
crown, and behind the ears. He smiles with the
anointment. He laughs when the water trickles
down his neck.

And then she combs. Pulling the wide teeth
against the scalp. Pouring oil until the strands
are thick and iridescent. Over and over Mata draws a
wooden comb through my father's hair. His
measured self.

urora

I shake my father awake.
He stirs and opens his eyes.
What is it, Jiva?

(*This* is my real name.)

Look.
I point outside.
He leans across me, presses his
face to the small plastic oval.

The sky shudders in coloured waves.

It's beautiful, he whispers.
Like a rainbow coming apart.

(Like a sari unwound.)

Peaceful.
His words brush the window.
She would have loved this.

He grips the paper-wrapped box
balanced on his left knee.
What remains of *she*.

We are bringing Mata home

In a box Bapu holds under his arm.
An urn. Brass.

He held it on his lap all the way
from Elsinore to Winnipeg.
One and a half hours on the bus.
On his lap in the taxi.
He can't bear to be away from her.

This is my wife, he explains to airport security.
Be careful with her. Her name is Leela.

The blond man in uniform hikes up his blue pants.
I don't care if her name is Sally-come-lately.

They x-ray her anyway. Someone shakes the box.
Can't be too careful these days.

My father stares angrily but says nothing. His
body is in pain as if it's his own heart they're
tossing.

This is my wife, he pleads with the flight attendant.

I understand, she says. *But for everyone's safety . . .*
He slides the box under the seat for takeoff.

I'm sorry, he whispers to my mother. *You should
never be at my feet.*

Dear Maya,
Watch over your father.
You will need each other.

Blame

Bapu is heavy with grief and remorse.
Blame too.

Where were you? Why did you leave your mother alone?
What were you doing that was more important than her?

I am not her caretaker! I shouted before running out
of the house into the fields.

My father claims Mata lost heart while waiting for
me.

> (What was she playing?
> The Bach that I loved?
> Schubert?
> No, it must have been
> Beethoven.)

And where was I?
Why didn't I rush home
like every other afternoon?

Because I had something to do.
I had to find out if my suspicions were right.

The piano

My father bought the piano when things got bad.

They're cheap in the country.
Every old farmhouse has one.
Always a piano for sale somewhere on the prairies.
Two hundred dollars.
And it's yours.

Mata insisted it be carried up the stairs to the
yellow wallpapered bedroom on the second floor.
The railing and a piece of a wall had to be
removed to make it fit. *I want it in a room with a
door*, she insisted.

It helped for a while. Instead of finding Mata
crying in the kitchen every afternoon, I came
home to music. The second-floor window
propped open. A waltz carried on the wind.

When she wasn't playing, she hummed. My father
and I exchanged smiles. Maybe this would help.
Forget the loneliness. Forget about going home.

But over the years, the music got louder. It was
angry, weeping, beautiful, and sad. I was
frightened and thrilled at the same time. She
played with such passion that I couldn't believe it
was my mother. This small quiet woman who sat

at dinner with her hands folded like an old-fashioned schoolgirl. Refusing food. Eyes staring ahead, always open, wet with tears. Even her weeping was controlled. But on the keyboard she was possessed.

Above the kitchen the floorboards groaned with music. Some days she even forgot and called me Jiva.

The day I heard Bapu weep at my mother's declaration, I knew things wouldn't get better.

There won't be another child, Amar, she said in English. *I have nothing to feed him.*

She put her hand on her breast
to show him it was flat.

My mother never spoke Punjabi again. Hindi became the language of her demise.

Beethoven

Piano Sonata no. 23 in F Minor.

Twenty-three minutes from the first to last touch
of her fingers on the keys. Twenty-three minutes
from the bus stop to home. Up the single-lane
gravel road into Mata's music.

I hear it before I see the window propped open
with a book. The melody escaping under the glass.
Winding between the trees, a grove of oaks, and
into the open fields. Like a scarf loosened from a
woman's neck, the music floats on air.

It is always Beethoven after 3:00.

The sonatas, Mata explains, *are my favourite. Four
movements. Like the four elements or the four
directions.*

The bus drops me at the end of our road and I run
North on the freshly-turned *Earth.*

But Beethoven's Appassionata *has only three
movements, Maya. The allegro assai is quick, lively
and cheerful. The andante con moto—attacca is
slower, hymn-like but still demanding to be listened to.
But the allegro, ma non troppo—presto is to be played
with passion. Like time is running out.*

If I leave the road and cross the pasture, I can catch the last.

There are only three. Like the stages of a life.

I pick up the pace, my feet springing out of the field's autumn stubble. The andante con moto calls to me. *Hurry*, the piano urges. *Run, Maya, run.*

When I reach the house, the last chords strike like prairie thunder and without a breath the allegro, ma non troppo begins. In the kitchen I kick my shoes into a dusty corner and take the stairs two at a time. At the top of the landing, a door swings open and I see Mata's long black braid swinging with the metronome. Arms fly out from her body, hands clawing the black and white keys. She plays as if the house might fall and only her music keeps it standing.

For the last two minutes, the sonata beats out my breaths. The music despairs. The building madness — the unhinged mind seeking order in music.

But there is something else too.

Something buried deep in the allegro, in the short melodic fragments. Is it love I hear? Not the sweet melody of early devotion when hearts cannot imagine their cracks, but a complex love: disappointments and betrayals tempered over time. Acceptance.

My parents had the most romantic love story

Like *Romeo and Juliet.* Warring families.
Montagues and Capulets. Khuranas and Dwivedis
plotting against each other, discouraging the
young lovers.

But Mata told me he looked like a warrior.
Tall and regal. A turban of molten bronze.

And my father, when pressed to remember,
says my mother glowed as if her body was the only
source of light in the hall. All shadows
disappeared. Then the rest of the world followed.

There was only her.

Leela. Meaning *"play."*

They meet at a wedding

A good omen according to my Hindu mother.
Auspicious. She is hiding behind a pillar ribboned
with green vines. Jasmine blossoms fill the hall
with honey sweetness.

No, it was the scent of your mother, Bapu insists.

His turban ought to have warned her away.
The families would never allow it. A marriage
between a Sikh and a Brahman would be full of conflicts.

But my mother is reckless. She rearranges her
sari. Silk the colour of a sunset. She steps from
behind the column and dares to look my
father straight in the eye.

From that moment on, he is lost.

Drowned, Mata had claimed.

Saved, Bapu says.

Or was it doomed?

The Courtship

For two months Leela is not allowed to leave the
house unaccompanied. Her mother warns,
You will be dead to me if you marry a Sikh.

In my father's house, his mother doesn't talk to
him for six weeks.

Actually, I enjoyed the quiet.

Bapu's father is not silent. He lectures that a
Sikh's duty is to God. His son's lust for the Brahman
girl will bring about my father's spiritual downfall.
He quotes the poet Bullashah:
    "Be content with thy circumstances,
    Do not be blinded by glamour,
    Fix thine attention on the seed,
    Ignore the branches, leaves, and fruit.
    That which comes and goes is transient,
    The wise do not become attached to it."

My father is not moved.
God is in his love for Leela.

My grandfather tries to scare my father.
My mother is an example of Maya,
the world of illusion, not the true world
of God. *A Sikh attached to Maya cannot escape
the cycle of life, death, and rebirth. Amar, you
will be bound to the Wheel of Existences!*

But the couple will not relent. They choose to believe that their parents' condemnation is for show. To save face, both families must express their displeasure at the union.

Three months later there is a wedding.
Leela holding his gaze.
My father rendered blind.

Amar. Means *"immortal."*

Dear Maya,
Love is like watching the approach of
one's beloved. Our hands reaching out.
A willingness to wait all eternity for the
touch.

At the Occasion of Bliss

The Sikh and Hindu families both celebrate.
They can't help themselves. All are swept up in the
wedding drama like a storm that blows in one
direction.

The groom arrives on horseback wearing a turban
of red. The couple walks around the sacred fire.
My father's scarf is tied to my mother's sari.

O God! I lovingly surrender to you.

To love each other is to love the Divine.

There are moments during the celebrations
when Mata's family whispers that
Sikhs are really just Hindus anyway. Just taller
and a bit arrogant. And lacking in religious
imagination.

Bapu's family whispers in kind that
Hindus are just un-evolved Sikhs. A people who
had yet to cast off their pantheon of gods and
goddesses. Still too romantic in their religious
philosophy.

But during the days of the wedding, they accept
each other's shortcomings. Families are united.
A peace is necessary.

And since the couple is emigrating, there will
be few reminders of the ill-thought marriage. They
will all go on as before. Ignoring the new relatives.

Before my parents leave for Canada, advice is
given: *Insist she become a Sikh*, my grandfather tells
his son. *Only then will you have real peace.*

Amar's answer: *I'll not step inside a temple without
her.*

My mother's family says nothing.
Leela is no longer their daughter.
Already dead to them.

What are you writing?

A family history.

Ah, Bapu says, looking down at the box on his lap.

He shifts in the narrow airplane seat, moving my
mother so she rests on his chest. He closes his eyes
and goes back to sleep.

The sky outside the window blackens like soot.
A nightmare erasing the colours of the wind.

We begin in Elsinore

Seventy-five miles southwest of Winnipeg. A
prairie town where sunflowers grow in neat, tall
rows. The sun drags the yellow faces from east to
west. The faithful adoration of the masses.

There are one thousand, four hundred, and
seventy-two Christian-like souls living in this
oddly named town. A Danish settler's choice? Or
a literary scholar who saw a castle in the clouds?

(Helen thinks a spinster English teacher crafted
the lofty name and then went slowly mad with small
town bordeom and the lack of marriageable men.)

There are also three pagans in this community.
That's us.

We rent an old farmhouse near the cemetery.

*(Just until we can buy our
own piece of land, Leela.)*

Bapu runs Jack's Mechanic Shop. A lease-to-own
deal negotiated with Jack's widow, Lucy, just
before she moved to Florida. My father's offer for
the shop was the only one.

Mata's job is to take care of the home, her
husband, a yard full of chickens, and two goats.
And me.

Cathy Ostlere 29

Fate

A man steps on the moon at the exact
moment I am born.

July 20, 1969. 9:56 p.m. (CDT)

When my mother learns this, she puts her lips
against my cheek and says, *Auspicious.*

I cry as if the man is walking over me
instead of the grey ash of Earth's satellite.

You will fly, Mata whispers.

My eyes are gelled. Closed like a kitten's.

Birth day

I arrive at the Brandon Hospital. Glistening like
the moon on a summer's night. Bapu says that I'm
so white I must be a changeling. A switch in the
womb. A fairy child. A delusion.

But Mata says, *Wait, Amar. It's just chalk dusting
her skin. The chalk from her story written across the
sky. The goddess Maya's hand is telling her future.*

Rubbish, Bapu says. *There is only one God.*

They are both surprised to hear Amar say this. He
has always been tolerant of Leela's beliefs. But
today, they hear the voice of his father.

Let me clean her, says the redheaded nurse. She
wipes away the sticky vernix, the chalk dust, the
story written in the clouds, and then I take my
proper colour.

The nurse holds me up for inspection. Bapu nods
his approval.

I am dark. Dark as Manitoban soil.
The earth he wants to own.

On the Eleventh day

Let's name her Neil.
After the astronaut.

You're delirious, Leela.

What about Luna?

No. My daughter will
not have a crazy name.

Then let's give her a Canadian-Indian name:
Strong-Arm-Swinging-at-Moon.

Are you mad? Did your brain fall
out with the baby? Listen, wife.
I have chosen a name.

What?

Jiva.

No, Amar! It's a boy's name.

It's a name for girls as well.

I will not name my daughter
after your father!

We'll talk about it later, Leela.
When you're back to normal.

We'll talk about it now!
The child should have a beautiful name.

It is beautiful!

It is a Sikh name.
It will offend my goddess.

Leela, there is only one God!

With the utterance of these words a second time,
my parents' world tilts on its axis. The horizon
moves. Somewhere a river floods over a field.
Islands are forming, drifting.

Maya. I will call her Maya, my mother whispers.
It is her destiny.

My father goes out the back door. His black eyes
red with anger. *Maya,* he spits. *Goddess of Illusion.*
Not reality.

He remembers what his father said:
    The world is a dream,
    Any moment it may pass away;
    Thou has built a house of sand,
    How can it endure?
    All this is Maya.

I should have listened and insisted you
become Sikh, Leela, or never married
you! That was your destiny!

Name

My birth certificate reads *Jiva*.
It means *"soul"* in Sanskrit.
But my mother privately called me Maya.
"Illusion." "Change." From Sanskrit too.

The truth of it —
what my two names really mean —
is that I was born into a division
that began long before me.

Munsa Devi

This is where we pray, Maya.
In Hindi. Not Punjabi.

(In the red barn
behind our house.)

This is our goddess.
Of desire.
And fertility.

(But I'm afraid of her.
And that snake in her hand.)

This is our altar.
And these are our gifts to her.
Water.
Fruit.
Incense.
Blue vermilion.
Golden turmeric.

Mata, is Munsa Devi married
to the man in Bapu's picture?

You mean Guru Nanak?

Yes. He is Sikh. She is Hindu.
Like you and Bapu.

Maya, never let your father hear
you ask that question.

Now on your knees.
Three times.
Every day.

Maya means "dream"

This is what my mother tells me when I'm five.
So dream away, Maya.

Her name is Jiva, Bapu says, rolling a piece of
chapati in his hand.

Why not Maya, Bapu? Why can't my name be Maya?

He sighs and leans close to my face.
Look at me, Jiva. What do you see?

Your beard?

What else?

My Bapu!

*Yes, your Bapu. But one day when you are older, you
will see that I was just a dream. And your mother too.
This life isn't real, Jiva. It's a veil that prevents us
from seeing the truth. The truth that is God's life.
This life is nothing but an illusion.*

He turns back to his food.

Amar! my mother shouts. *You're scaring the child.*

She needs to know the truth, Leela.

She's five!

Maya means "Delusion," *Leela. Maya is what a Sikh tries to escape from during his life on earth.* He pushes away from the table.

But why do you want to escape from me?

Not you, Maya. I mean not you, Jiva. The point is one can only attain spiritual enlightenment by escaping the trance of Maya.

Mata picks me up in her arms and argues back:
One can also attain spiritual enlightenment through compassion.

Your name is Jiva, Bapu says, as the screen door slams behind him. *Don't forget.*

Dear Maya,
Life is an illusion.
And as it turns out, so is death.
What is real?
What remains when we all fade away?
Two things: Love. Forgiveness.
Don't forget.

October 29-30, 1984

Home

India bubbles like lava.
Waves of heat stir the air into water.
Black asphalt turns to pitch.
The plane lands on the soft grey tarmac and sinks.

Bapu puts his turban on his head.
Balances Mata's ashes on his lap.
He sighs and whispers, *We're home.*

He's not talking to me.

We've arrived

Not yet to Chandigarh, *City Beautiful*, where
Mata's sisters weep and wail for the mourning
month, not yet to the Golden State of Punjab and
its angry air, but New Delhi. City of stink and
noise. Streets clogged with flesh. Voices loud and
soft.

Sounding of despair.

Smelling of pee.

No eat no eat

hungry

a one-armed woman pleads

hungry

her invisible hand

rupees

finds my arm

rupees

paws and paws

no eat

gives me shivers

give me rupees

her eyes are saucers

no eat one week

her skull a moon

hungry

white bone

hungry

white stone under skin

Look away, Jiva, Bapu says.

But I can't.

no eat no eat

her children whimper

no eat no eat

sing their song of hunger

no eat no eat

with bellies swollen

like party balloons

Look away. You can't help them.

the mother bares her breast

a shriveled apple of sustenance

Look.
Away.

Rickshaw rickshaw

rickshaw rickshaw
you want rickshaw

No rickshaw, Bapu says to the small brown
man, but he pretends not to hear.

where you go
where you go

The man's skin is dry.
Veined and lined like leather.

my rickshaw fast
very very fast

His body twists and writhes,
coils around Bapu's arm.

good price
just for you
returning son of India

My father has brought me to a
country where snakes can talk.

where you go
I take you
come come

NO RICKSHAW, Bapu shouts at the man.
He shrinks to the ground, hissing.

good price

Chai

A hand tugs at my arm
holds up a small earthen cup.

chai chai

It belongs to a boy, small,
yet his face is old. He could be
nine or twenty or thirty-seven.

one rupee chai

He puts the chai into my hand,
presses my fingers around
the unbaked clay.

drink now chai chai

The tea is brown like a puddle.

one rupee

And swirling like an eddy.

chai rupee rupee chai

I hear voices rising out of the cup.

chai rupee rupee

Crying.

chai rupee rupee chai

Weeping.

chai rupee chai chai

Like crows plucked alive.

eat rupee rupee eat
aiii hungry rupee chai

The air rings with longing
and pain.

aiii rupee aiii rupee

The ground shakes with heartbreak

and sorrow.

aiii rupee aiii chai

I raise the cup to my lips.

aiii aiii aiii

The tea slides down my throat
and I swallow India.

Don't ever leave my side!

Bapu grabs my arm and
the cup falls.

why you drop chai

It breaks into pieces.

you pay me one rupee

Clay shards returned to dust.

now now you pay me

But I am dragged away.

you pay you pay

Before I can pay.

Keep walking, Jiva, and close your ears.

But I cannot close my ears.

aiii aiii

The voices seep in.

aiii aiii

Spilled tea darkening the earth.

aiii aiii

A hungry chorus.

eat

Swallowing me.

eat eat

Until I am one of them.

aiii

Wanting.

hungry

Needing.

eat rupee rupee

We are sick in our wanting and need.

Don't listen! Bapu shouts above the crowd.

eat rupee rupee chai

Don't listen?
That's the answer?

eat eat rupee rupee

Don't listen to hunger?
Don't listen to pain?

A bony hand reaches out and claws
my father's arm. A woman swings a
skinny baby close to his face.

a week a week
no eat a week

He stops.
Looks into the mother's eyes.
Her tears run flat streams.

Then eat your children, Bapu says.

Who are you?

What would you have me do, Jiva?
Feed all the starving?
Buy them artificial limbs?
Buy their children?

No. Of course not, I shout back.
Just see them.
See their pain.
Acknowledge their suffering.

I am tired of pain, he says.

He grabs my hand.
Pulls me through the crowd.
I know I'm stepping on people's feet.

And besides, there's nothing we can do, Jiva.
Perhaps they'll do better in their next life.

But I think he means they should have
done better in their last.

Karma.

Returning son of India

I don't know this side of my father.
Cold.
Detached.
Cruel.
Walking proudly
past the poor,
the hungry,
the wounded,
the amputees of limb and soul.

Returning son of India.
How can he not see?

At home, he notices every person on the street.

(Their stares. Their
downward glances.)

He smiles awkwardly and says hello.
He touches his turban, the nervous tick
of forefinger to the temple.
He never puts his hand out first.

But here, he's different.
Confident.
Even strutting.
Is this his true home?

This country where he doesn't
stick out like a sore thumb?

Home.
A place where no one stares.
And no one cares.

Dear Maya,
It's not easy to live in a country far from
where you're born. It's not easy to go home.

Overheard on Main Street, Elsinore

- *You know the country's going to shit when they let the towel-heads in.*

- *I heard he hides a knife under that hat.*

- *And I heard he gives away a free carpet when you buy a set of tires!*

- *Hey, Amar! Hope your head gets better soon!*

- *Leave him alone, boys. You'll need Mr. Singh when your tractor breaks down.*

Overheard at the I.G.A. grocery store

- It's called a sari.

- It must be hard to walk in.

- Do you think it's only for going out?

- For shopping in Elsinore? Kind of fancy for these parts.

- Bob was in their house last week, you know,
  and he said she wears it at home too.

- How would you do housework with that end
  flung over the shoulder?

- I hear the old Franz place smells of curry.
  Real spicy. Jack must be turning over in his grave.

- Do you think it's made of silk?

- I hear they're rich. Used to have servants.
  Look at her jewelry. It's all gold, you know.

- Well, if they're that well-off, what are they
  doing in Elsinore? Who in their right mind
  would move here?

The Sari Emporium

You must have something to wear, Bapu insists
as he pushes open a door on Arya Samaj Road.
The din of traffic fades away.

He means: something to wear to meet the relatives
who only know me from photographs.

You must look Indian or they will not like you.

(Like I care.)

There are no Indian clothes in my suitcase at
the hotel. I packed only jeans and T-shirts.
Bapu shouted loudly when he discovered
this fact too late.

They'll think you're a Western whore!

*Well, Bapu, you're the one who encouraged Mata
to wear pants and where has that gotten us?*

I thought he might hit me.

(A first for me. Helen says
she's smacked regularly.)

But Bapu didn't touch me. Instead his face turned
grey and he walked out of the hotel room without
saying a thing.

I wanted to yell like Mata used to: *Go ahead, leave me alone here. What do you care for how my life is?* But instead, I just lay on the bed and cried.

Silk

Inside the air-conditioned store, the staff of young
women flutter around me like pretty birds. Their
bracelets shake. They smile. Touch my clothes.
Stroke my wavy unoiled hair that I refused to
braid this morning.

See the scene you've caused, Bapu says under his
breath.

Because of my jeans.

> (Because I tore up all my
> saris after Mata died.)

Because they know we're not from here.

> (Orange silk blowing in an
> open prairie window.)

I shall have to pay more now.

When the saleswomen start draping silks over my
head, Bapu waves his hand like he's about to hit
them with an open palm. They bow deeply and
retreat to the shadows.

One size fits all

Anyone can wear a sari, Mata used to tell me.
One size fits all. Hindus, Sikhs, Christians.
Even Muslims. Many Sikh women wear a *salwar
kameez,* a loose-fitting pant and long top, but my
mother preferred the sari. She thought the *salwar
kameez* was too similar to North American
pyjamas.

I'll not be laughed at, she told her new husband,
shortly after they arrived in Canada in 1968.

Amar had let it go. *Wear what you want. This
country is so young it doesn't matter. The streets are
filled with immigrants like ourselves. There's no such
thing as a real Canadian anyway except for the
Indians. And we're Indians!* He thought this was
very funny.

Leela looked on Elsinore's Main Street for women
like herself and saw none. The women wore short
dresses, their pale calves sticking out like the thin
legs of flightless birds. Some wore pants.
Everyone stared at her sari. In the beginning she
thought they were just jealous. Canadian clothes
were lumpy and stiff.

Reena's Sari Shop in Winnipeg

The sari is five thousands years old, Mata says, as I
crawl under a table of coloured waterfalls spilling to
the floor. *As old as Sanskrit text.*

Mata's eyes are closed. Her fingers graze.
Silks from Banaras, Mysore. Synthetics with
pretty names. Georgette. Chiffon. *Kanjeevaram*
saris. The longest and heaviest. Embroidered with
real gold.

Mata can always tell the difference.

*There hasn't been a woman born that can't be made
beautiful by wearing a sari. It softens our bones.*

According to Mata, the value of a sari lies in how
it falls from the body. The drape from the waist.
Small hand-gathered folds. The detailed *pallu*
flowing down a woman's back like a Himalayan
river.

*Weight is very important when choosing cloth. The eye,
our most unreliable sense, is often seduced by gold
threads, or fooled by sheen or variegated threads. But
weight is honest. It doesn't change with the light or
one's mood. How much air can pass through the
weave? Is the cloth heavy and dense like the earth or
thin, resembling the wind itself?*

From under the table I watch her drape the sari
like a veil.

Maya! Where are you?

I crawl out from my hiding place.

Why are saris so long, Mata?

I'll tell you when you're older.

The one

Bapu leaves me alone.

I browse between the stacks of fabric.
Searching with my hands.

I know it's there, but I can't rush over the lesser
fabrics. I must touch slowly. Respect the blends
and rayons. Starched cotton. Not all can be silk.

I wander through the garden. My hands caress
brocades heavy as canvas. I could do this blind.
I know weight like Mata.

When I finally find it, I stroke gently, afraid it will
disintegrate like tissue. I feel the golden birds fly in
a delicate filigree. Wings as light as clouds.

I lift the sari under my face and glance at the
mirror.
   "Tall, short, skinny, fat,
   rich or poor we fold and wrap."

You look like your mother, Bapu says, appearing
beside me. *On her wedding day.*

The glow of red silk.

Helen of Elsinore

Helen likes singing Mata's dressing song:
Tall, short, skinny, fat,
rich or poor we fold and wrap.

I drape my blue sari over her
head and shoulders.

Helen, I think you look like Mother Mary
in the Christmas play.

Great. A pregnant virgin. I wish I had a sari. Then we
could both wear them to school . . . where they would
accidentally unravel in front of Michael! And he'd go
crazy trying to decide which one of us he desired more!

I glare at Helen, but she just giggles
and mouths S-E-X-Y.

I'm still trying to forget that moment.

> (Michael helping me stand up.
> The end of my sari pooling in his
> hands. *Sorry,* he whispered.)

Really? You want to forget Michael Divienne leaning
over your body in the middle of the hallway?

What?

Focus, Jiva. Focus.

You focus, Helen. We're supposed to be doing our project on world religions. You're the Christian. I'm the weird Sikh.

Fine. Helen pulls a green sari around her hips like it's a beach towel. *Tell me again what you believe in, Jiva?*

Maya, a voice whispers from the hallway.

Did you say something? Helen asks.

*Tall, short, skinny, fat
rich or poor we fold and wrap.*

My mother's voice floats through the open bedroom door.

Hello, Mrs. Singh! How are you?

I usher Helen past Mata, pushing her into the bathroom. *We believe that we have many lives, Helen.* I lock the door. *If we live well, we are rewarded in our next life.*

And if you mess up?

You're a cockroach.

Cool, Helen says, while examining the clumps in her mascara. *Reincarnation. Another chance.*
Every one deserves a second chance, don't you think?

My mother hears only music

The piano fallboard slams shut.

What did you say? Mata's mouth is trembling.

Nothing, Mata. Please don't stop playing.

What. Did. You. Say.

*I said that when you play, your fingers are quick. They
run like the mice run in the barn. But I meant . . .
happy mice.*

*Yes. Mice. I play music for chickens, cows, and sleeping
cats. And my daughter says my hands are like rodents.*

I watch my mother's beautiful hands flutter above
her head as if she's playing a piano suspended in
air. At the tips of her fingers, the short white nails
glow like opals.

Suddenly Mata grabs my arm and drags me down
the stairs to the kitchen. She pulls on the heavy
back door, then kicks the screen open with her foot,
pushing me into the pale sunlight. In the summer,
startled chickens would have flown up cackling in a
panic. In the fall, I would have heard a combine
coughing clouds of black smoke in the fields. But in

the winter, there isn't a sound. The prairie is
silent. Like the inside of an egg.

Tell me what you hear, Maya?

My shoulders shake under her hands. I want to
say the right thing, the thing that will take away
her anger, the thing that will make her smile and
not feel so alone. I want to say I hear music. I
hear Bach when I'm feeding the chickens. I hear
Beethoven like it's my own heartbeat. I hear music
all around me. *Your music, Mata.* But it's
pointless. There is only one answer to this
question.

I hear the wind, I whisper. Mata lifts her clenched
hands from my shoulders, looking at them as if
they no longer belong to her. *It's what I always
hear.*

My mother looks up at the sky brushed with long
white clouds like a horse's tail. *If I'm lucky, Maya,
your wind will carry me away one day.* She steps
inside the house, her hand pulling the screen door
tight against the spring-loaded latch. Then she
closes the wooden door and turns the lock.

Sometimes the wind says my name. It whispers,
Maya.

Who has seen the wind?

"Neither you nor I:
But when the trees bow down their
heads
The wind is passing by."

Mrs. Robinson had us learn Rossetti's poem in the third grade. And then we went outside to look for evidence.

We stood in the playground at Elsinore Elementary, staring at the fields. Twenty-one eight-year-olds, eyes peering. Waiting for the wind to bend the stalks.

There, there it is! I shouted. *The wind is orange!*

No, honey, the teacher said. *We can't really see the wind, only its movement.*

But I can see it, I said.

No, you can't, some of the others jeered. *You're just pretending.*

But I wasn't. High in the air, above the turned heads of the sunflowers, a broad orange ribbon floated through the air.

Their laughter reminded me of what I already
knew. I was different. I had strange parents that
came from a place far away. Across an ocean, a
world of turbans and saris and peculiar alphabets.
I came from a people who saw things that weren't
really there. We made worlds out of nothing: air,
wind, water, revenge.

But Helen, the prettiest girl in the class, envied me.

If I could see the wind, I'd know where to hide, she whispered.
*My father has a bad temper. He hits me just because I don't
like peas!*

She took my hand. I had a friend who needed to
disappear too.

Overheard through the bedroom walls

No one in town ever
talks to me, Amar.

> *Then you must talk first.*
> *Be friendly.*
> *It takes time.*

Time? We've lived here nine years.

> *You have to try harder.*

Why should I have to be the one to
try so hard? Do you know that one day
a woman actually reached out and touched
my sari? Like I was a bolt of fabric in a store.
Such rudeness.

> *Then wear a dress.*
> *Some pants.*
> *Leave the sari for home.*

Never. Canadian clothes are hideous.
They are little better than a scarecrow's.
Would you consider not wearing your turban?

> *That's different.*

Oh, yes, Amar. That's different.
If you're a man. If you're a Sikh.
I'm just a Hindustani woman in this
godforsaken place.

> *You must learn to hold*
> *your head high, Leela.*

I can't any longer.
Their eyes burn
through my skin.

I feel like I must apologize
and I don't even know for what!

> *Well, then stay home.*
> *And never go out*
> *again if that pleases you.*

I can't live like this, Amar.
You must take me home.

> *There's no money, Leela.*
> *The shop needs new tools.*

Then just one ticket.
Please.

> *You'd leave your daughter*
> *and husband behind?*

For a visit, Amar.
A few months.
That's all.

> *Stop these selfish thoughts, Leela!*
> *Your life is here.*

But this isn't a life!
It's a slow death.

My mother cries all night.
My father paces the floor.
I pull the bedcovers over my head
so I don't have to listen to any more.

All in good time

Mrs. Hart, my homeroom teacher, always says
this. *We must have patience. Good things come to
those who wait.*

The class sits still. Backs straight. Hands clasped
in front on top of the desks. Everyone trying not
to breathe. A breath could sink us.

All in good time, she says softly as her hips swivel
up the aisle like two pivoting pumpkins.

I can't look at this, Michael groans, loud enough so
even the first row can hear.

Helen giggles and then stuffs her fist into a
perfectly outlined pink lip-sticked mouth. I look at
her admiringly. This is the girl who became my
best friend the day she said: *Don't ever cut your hair,
Jiva. I'll just kill you.*

Patience, Mrs. Hart repeats. *When you are all
perfectly still, I will dismiss you. I can stay here all day,
you know.*

I'll just bet she could, Michael mutters behind me.
P-p-p-patience, Jiva. His lips are close. His breath.
On my neck. *Patience, girl. Some things are worth
waiting for.* His words sear my skin.

Patient

That's the English word my father uses with my
mother.

*We must be patient, Leela. We'll go back to Punjab at
the right time. Maybe there will be another child yet, if
God wills it. Maybe a boy.*

Oh, yes, Amar. We all must wait for your God's will.

She leaves the room. Beethoven bangs overhead.

I try to be patient too.

(Not about a visit to Punjab.

Who cares?)

Not foreign

I must wait for Michael to notice me.
Not my colour.
Not my sari.
Not someone in a play
dressed in costume.
But me.

> (The *me* who wouldn't
> be foreign with *him*.)

In the beginning
I smiled at him all the time
even when he ignored me.
I started to help him with math.
I laughed at his lame jokes.

> (Three naked nuns and a
> man selling window blinds
> isn't really that funny.)

Then Helen got involved.

Don't look so interested, she said.
Boys hate girls who are interested.
No. No. No. You can't help him with homework.
Tell him you didn't do so well on the last test.
Boys hate smart girls.

> (Really?)

So I ignored Michael.

Pretended he didn't exist.
And sure enough
he began to tease me.

Good morning, Rikki-tikki-tavi!

And I didn't even mind.

(Why am I so stupid?)

I thought I was lucky.
To have a friend like
Helen teaching to me how
to control my desires.

Men like to be in control, she instructed.
If you push too hard, they just turn away.

My mother had no friends to teach her this.
No one to advise her on husbandly behaviour.
If she had, I think Mata would have been out
the kitchen door in under three seconds, stealing for
the airport, in a car driven by a friend.

Overheard in our kitchen

You Sikhs are just so full of pride,
Amar. Your gurus, your symbols,
your one God! You believe you're
better than the rest of us.

If we seem proud, Leela, it's because
we have much to be proud about.
We believe in tolerance and
acceptance of all faiths. We believe
all beings are equal. We believe
women should have equal status.
We believe in truth and justice. We
believe the use of force is a last
resort.

And love, Amar?

Yes, I am proud of my love for you.

See? You think you're
doing me a favour!

It was God who brought
us together, Leela.

Really? What was He thinking?

Mata is crying day and night

Don't you miss your homeland,
Amar? The broad plains? The fields
of wheat? Our Punjab of the five
rivers?

> *No.*

What about our families?

> *You have no family, Leela, except*
> *mine. If we go back, we will live*
> *with my father and mother. Do you*
> *think you can do that? My father*
> *will insist you become Sikh. There*
> *will be no altar to your goddess.*

We can live alone.
As we do here, Amar.

> *We cannot live alone*
> *and insult my parents.*

So we live here and
insult me instead?

> *Leela, we came here to get away*
> *from my father and his narrow*
> *beliefs. You still have your* puja.
> *And Jiva is learning about both*
> *religions.*

But I have no one to pray with, but a
daughter who won't dress Indian
unless it's Halloween! I have
religious freedom but no community.

So what does it matter? Perhaps it
would be better to be a slave in
another woman's house than be
lonely in your own.

No. I worship my mother, Leela,
but I love you. My mother will
treat you badly. And I will be
unable to stop it. Here, at least,
you are under no one's thumb.

But we're not meant to live so alone.
Perhaps even hatred is better than
this isolation, Amar.

Hatred is a form of isolation,
Leela. Look around at this
country. These rivers. These
fields. These deep blue skies.
There's peace all over this land.
No blood in the soil to stain our
lives. No families to tell us how to
be.

It's not home.

It's better.

It's empty.

It's free.

I'll never be free here. I belong
nowhere. All my gods and goddesses
have disappeared.

Dear Maya,
You've never seen a man stare at the sky and
earth for so long. He thought that in this
country, love would be enough.

So, what's so great about being a Sikh?

I used to like this about Helen.
Never afraid to ask the tough
questions. Even while Madonna
rolled across the MTV stage in
white tulle.

Like a virgin, Helen sang along.
Touched for the very first time. Like
a vir-r-r-r-gin. Hey, Jiva, what
religion do you suppose she is?

It was the last time we laughed together.

Are you thinking of changing
religions, Helen?

Yes. Either to yours or
hers. The clothes are better.

Okay. Here's how it works. Sikhs
believe in one God. Like you. If you
believe in anything at all. But their goal
in life is not to enter heaven through
salvation but to be united with God
completely. Human and divine as one.

Cosmic sex?

No. Through truth. And good
behaviour.

And tell me again how
many lives it takes?

Until one is willing to give up the
desires of the physical world.

So forever then.
But it's different
for Hindus, right?

Well, same problem of rebirth. But
more choice of gods and goddesses.
My mother worships Munsa Devi.

Who wrote the Kama Sutra?

Helen, seriously.

Sorry. I know. Have you ever
tried to imagine your parents
doing it.

No! And why would you want to?

Yuck.

The break-up

*Anything else you'd like to know,
Helen?*

*Tell me about the goddesses.
I promise no more jokes.*

*There are hundreds of thousands of
divine beings in Hindusim. But they
all represent an aspect of the
Supreme Being called Permatma,
who is the ultimate reality.*

The ultimate reality. *Very
dramatic. Especially with the
saris and the no-cutting-hair
thing, and some of you covering
your heads and faces.*

*It's Muslim women who
cover their faces, Helen!*

Millions.

But there are Muslims in India?

*You know, Christianity is dreary by
comparison. You get one life. There's
one man on a cross who can save your
soul. No colourful clothing or hidden
knives or men with hair down to the
ground. We are dull dull dull.*

*Honestly, it's not all it's
cracked up to be.*

*Maybe. But your family looks
passionate. Romantic. Like royalty.*

We live with goats and
chickens, like you, Helen!

But you get to wear a sari!

Michael still talks about it, you
know. He thinks it's sexy. And
mysterious. Like a strange cult with
blood and sex rituals.

You talk to Michael
about my clothes?

Well, not all of your clothes.
The regular ones you wear to
school are kind of boring.

Helen, I don't want you
talking to Michael about
anything that has to do with me.

Fine. I've been trying to help you
get together with him, but if you
don't want it, that's okay.

Well, if Michael likes me so
much, why doesn't he talk
instead of always whispering
behind my ear? He's not mute.
Especially with you.

What's that supposed to mean?
Michael and I are just friends! You
know that! Tell you what, Jiva. Get
a boyfriend your own way. God
knows you're so gorgeous you
shouldn't need my help.

The promise

One night Mata exacted a promise from Bapu.

All right, all right! We'll go back to India when Jiva is sixteen!

My mother smiled. My father slammed the door.
I shrugged. India was far away and so was my
birthday. At least a year.

But who could have predicted what would happen
next?

That Punjab would become a place of turmoil and
violence.

That a movement would grow: Sikhs
demanding a homeland called Khalistan.

That Sikh terrorists would begin murdering
anyone who wouldn't toe the line.

And that Indira Gandhi, the Indian prime minister,
would send the army into the Golden Temple in
Amritsar, violating the Sikh holy site.

India was unraveling along religious lines.

The Partition of 1947

It cannot happen again, Bapu said.
*More than a million died when the country split
in two. Those wounds are still not healed.*

I knew my history. That was the year that
India and Pakistan became their own
nations and created borders according to
religion. More than half of the area known
as Punjab went to the new Islamic state of
Pakistan. The land that remained in India
was eventually divided into three new
Indian states: Haryana, Himachal
Pradesh, and Punjab.

Punjab was for the Punjabi speakers.
Half were Sikhs.

*Indira Gandhi will never allow Punjab to
separate,* Bapu explained. *Because it borders
Pakistan.*

*Indira Gandhi will never be able to stop the
Sikhs from trying,* Mata said. *And what will
happen to all the Hindus in Punjab?*

My mother then cried when she realized
what it meant for her.

How will we go home now, Amar? Sikhs and
Hindus being driven apart. Where does that
leave us?

Our marriage is a symbol of peace, Leela.
Don't forget.

Amar, we live in a country where no one knows
what a Sikh is. In Canada, we symbolize
nothing. In India, we just look like fools.

October 31–November 1, 1984

Madness in New Delhi

Bapu brings the news in the dark.

I open the hotel door to his frantic rapping.
His face pours sweat, the vein over his left eye
throbbing like molten lava moving under the skin.

He grips my arm with one hand, but it is weak. He
pushes me back from the window, and with the
other hand flicks off the light. The room is lit by a
streetlamp, a false moon glowing placidly.

He is breathing hard.

We're safe. This part of the city is still untouched.

Untouched from what? I ask.

He paces the floor, touching his turban, the
nervous tick of forefinger to the temple.

*They're crying for vengeance, Jiva. There are stories of
unspeakable things.*

I feel the heat where Bapu holds me. The
ligaments in his arm tighten, cling like metal
clamps. The blue arched veins on the back of his
hand swell like damned rivers.

What things, Bapu?

*The words "blood for blood" are singing through the city.
Mobs of men are pulling Sikh men out of buses, off
scooters, out of their homes. They are beating the bodies,
hacking off the limbs. They are burning turbans in the
street, soaked in oil. They make necklaces of burning
tires. And that's not all. They are raping Sikh women.
They are castrating young boys. Squeezing the organs of
life until they split. Like a cracked watermelon spilling
seeds and red juice.*

This is what happened

Halloween.

The prime minister of India is wearing an orange sari as she walks in the garden at No. 1 Safdarjung Road, in the city of New Delhi. Along the gravel path she meets two of her bodyguards.

She folds her hands in the morning light and says, *Namaste.* The two Sikh guards do not greet her in the usual fashion with a deep bow. Instead, one answers with three shots from a .38 revolver. The other with thirty rounds from a Sten automatic.

The power of the bullets lifts her body off the ground and spins her around. Twenty-seconds of pelting rain. A monsoon of certain death.

She falls when the firing stops. 9:17 a.m.

The assassins drop their weapons next to bone and flesh splattered on the ground. One of them addresses a security guard: *I've done what I had to do. You do what you have to do.* Both are shot, but only one is killed.

When the physician at the All India Institute of Medical Sciences receives the woman's body, he says: *This cannot be Indira Gandhi. She looks like a*

child wrapped in a washerman's sheet. Is this really the
Prime Minister of India?

A rumour begins that her heart remained intact.
Not a shot on the mark.

A contrary rumour says a single bullet found
its way to the muscle.

By nightfall in New Delhi, a city cries for the old
woman shot thirty-three times in her garden.

In Punjab, they are dancing in the streets.

In our hotel room, Bapu moans behind a locked
door knowing what will come.

His voice is the same

As the night Mata died.
The same tremor.
A stringed instrument wound too tight.

Oh my God. My God.

Bapu talks fast.
Believes he is holding down my fear.

Don't worry, Jiva.
It'll be all right.
The madness can't last long.
Or can it?
Oh, who knows with Indians.
Give them a reason to stir up their hate and off they go.
Poking at old wounds.
Remember! Remember! They shout.
Injustice! Injustice!

His voice is the same as the night Mata died.
The quiet room. Freezing air. Piano keys stilled,
bared like white teeth. Her sari whispering,
fluttering in the open window.

He broke the silence with his cries.

Oh, why, Leela? Why?
We were supposed to be enough for each other!

After that Bapu didn't stop talking for two weeks.
His words strung like beads on a ribbon.
Connected by a relentless tongue. Sometimes he
sang. Songs I had never heard. Prayers of grief.
Sorrowful laments.

I wondered if he was afraid of his thoughts. Stop
talking and you hear the other voices. The ones in
your head. The ones you ignored. The ones you
shushed.

I can't go on like this, Amar.
I will die from the loneliness.

And now it's the same in New Delhi.
As if talking keeps his panic at bay.

Jiva Jiva Jiva we will have to find a way out of here out
of Delhi far away because we can't stay here not safe
not safe but where where can we go perhaps a train a
bus no no everyone will think a train a bus they will
expect that wait for us no we will have to be sneaky we
will have to hide but where where with Kiran yes Kiran
will help us yes Kiran will help

Tonight he uses only English. Abandoning the
language of his childhood. Words linking him to a
murder.

After Mata died, English was banned from our
house. *Canada killed her,* he said in Punjabi.

The Golden Temple

Bapu says her death
is due to architecture.

Because a four-hundred- year-old
temple was desecrated.

(Because of the wind that
came through the cracks
in an old prairie house.)

Because its doors were entered
(East. West. North. South.)
without respect.

(Because the back door
never closed properly.)

Because the gold was tarnished
with blood.

(Because the kitchen was
always cold. And empty.)

Because of hate. Prejudice.
Intolerance.

(Because of love.)

Because the extremists used the
temple for a sanctuary of violence.

(Because it wasn't home.)

Architecture inspires and kills.

Darkening

Rumours are becoming believed facts:

- Sikhs are distributing sweetmeats and lighting oil
  lamps to celebrate Mrs. Gandhi's death.

- Trains are arriving from Punjab. Filled
  with Hindus murdered by Sikhs.

We will never be forgiven, Bapu says. For these lies.

Blood for blood!

Khoon ka badla khoon!

Marauding gangs search the districts
of New Delhi for turbaned men:

Munirka
Saket
South Extension
Lajpat Nagar
Bhogal
Jangpura
Asharm
Connaught Circle

Beating and burning as they go.

A red-painted *X* marks the spot
where Sikhs can be found:

In their houses.
In their shops.
In their temples.

Even the gurudwaras, Bapu cries.
Is no place safe?

Despair

Sikh men are cutting hair
shaving beards
removing turbans
as if they never mattered
at all.

Shorn

No, Bapu. Not your hair.

                            I'm a marked man, Jiva.

But what about God?

                           He'll have to understand.

You will be patit,
I cry into his shoulder.
No longer a Sikh.

                      A Sikh man must be more than
                      his hair. He is his word and his
                      belief. And if I'm dead, Jiva,
                      what good is my word?

I remember Mata washing my father's
hair. The river flowing through her
small hands.

Please don't, Bapu.

                      Listen, Jiva. I must keep you
                      safe and I can't looking like this.
                      Now cut it!

He puts a pair of silver scissors into my hand.
(Where did they come from?) I have never
held anything so heavy in my life.

You are asking me to kill
what is most precious to you.

I am asking you to save
my soul and my daughter.

The blades cut through the night.
But not easily. Even they resist,
dulled by sorrow.

Bapu sings. A battle prayer.

Daiwo Shiva Bar Mohay Aihoo —

The hair falls to the floor.
My father weeps. For all that he has lost.

I cry too. As Hindu and Sikh.

Help

I want you to wait here. I'll be back as soon as I can.

His hand rises, the nervous tick of forefinger to the temple. He is startled and then remembers why the turban is gone. Fingers run through the short stiff spikes, my handiwork.

I'm going to go and get help, Jiva. In the Mangolpuri district. Kiran Sharma lives there. He'll help us get out of Delhi. Or hide us.

(We are criminals.
We are fugitives.)

Is he Hindu?

Yes. An old friend from university. A highly moral man who doesn't believe in violence.

Sometimes friends change, you know, Bapu.

(A stolen sari.
A stolen kiss.)

Not this man. He lives a life devoted to tolerance. And we are close friends like you and Helen.

My throat tightens. Like me and Helen?

*Let me come with you, Bapu. I don't want to be left
here.*

*I can go faster alone, Jiva, and you'll be safer here. You
heard what they're doing to the women. I can't take
the chance.*

But what if you're seen?

*I'll stay out of sight. In the shadows. Or I will blend
in. I don't think I look Sikh any longer without my hair.*

I look at him. His hair won't lie down even with
the coconut oil. His beard has been trimmed, but
there was no razor to shave it close. I don't know
if he looks Sikh or not, but if someone stands close,
they will see the fear in his eyes.

What should I do if you don't come back?

I will. I promise, Jiva.

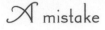 mistake

There's something I have to
tell you, Jiva. Before I go.

His hands hold his head.
The heavy weight. Of sorrow?
Or something else?

What is it, Bapu?

I made a terrible mistake in
bringing you here.

But how were you to know someone would
kill the prime minister? We had to bring
Mata's ashes. I understand.

No, not that.
There's another thing.

The nervous tick.
Though the turban is gone.

What other thing, Bapu?

The great desire.
Of your mother.

What desire?

For you to have a husband.

I know that.

An Indian husband.

I know that too.

An Indian husband in India.

In India?
She never said India!

I'm sorry, Jiva.

The hands. The head.

But you can't mean now!

I know. I know.

You brought me to India
to leave me here?

His fingers shake. Search
for his hair, his beard.

Your mother's wish, Jiva.

My hands are fists.
The nails pierce my palms.

So Amar Singh will give away his
daughter because he couldn't make his
wife happy!

I thought she'd get
used to Canada.

Don't talk to me.
(Not even sixteen.)

I thought there would
be more children.

Don't talk to me.

(A husband.)

I didn't listen to her.
It's my fault.

Don't talk!
(Sex with a stranger.)

Please, Jiva.
Forgive me for everything.

(Sold! For the price
of a father's guilt!)

Red sari

And now I remember.

That one is only for brides, the saleslady
at the sari shop had whispered.

While I was touching the
red silk, Bapu had smiled
at me. He was imagining
my worst nightmare.

A marriage to a man I'd never met.
The wedding night:
The sari slip pushed up my thighs.
The husband forcing his body into mine.
And later:
The mother-in-law checking the bedsheets.
For proof of virginity.
My reluctant and conquered blood.

What is happening to my life?

Oh, Mata. Do you see what your actions have
done to me? Or was this always your plan?

Dear Maya,
We cannot see how our lives will unfold.
What is destiny and what is accident?
And how can one ever be certain?

Leaving

Bapu gets up and walks to the door. His eyes rest on Mata's urn. Then he pulls them away to look at me for what seems like an eternity. *Be ready, Jiva.* He turns the handle. Steps into the hall, ducking under the doorframe. An old habit. Now, without the turban, it's no longer necessary.

I've always thought of my father as tall, taller than most, but tonight he has shrunk. To half the man.

I let him go. Not even a kiss on his cheek. And not a word. A good daughter would have accepted his apology.

I turn the lock and lean my back against the door. The turban is tossed on the bed. It looks like a giant seashell abandoned by its former inhabitant.

The empty home.

Questions

I didn't ask him.
Am I betrothed to a Sikh or a Hindu man?
Or just a boy?

Because a Sikh would make
Mata furious. And a Hindu
would make Bapu ill. But how
deep is my father's guilt?

And there's something else I
didn't ask him: Why is it when
Mata was alive, we couldn't
afford to fly to India?

It's really all you had to do,
Bapu. Take your wife home once in
a while. And maybe she wouldn't have
gone crazy. And we wouldn't be here.
And my father wouldn't be running in
the darkness with a bare head.
And I wouldn't be alone. My life
falling apart so spectacularly

Shhh

I am to stay quiet.

Don't open the door, Jiva.
Don't answer the telephone.

Let no one know I am here.

Stay away from the window.

It is dangerous to be seen and heard.

Don't speak.

Not a sound.

Remember. No one should know you are here.

Without a voice, I am safe?

A shiver climbs up the steps of my spine. What does
Helen's mother say? *Someone is walking over your grave.*

(Someone is taking
my hand in marriage.)

I feel cold.

(Someone is kissing
the boy that I like.)

I pull Mata's sari over my shoulders.
Orange. Mrs. Gandhi wore orange too.

ire

I close my eyes and see the prime minister's body
shattered on her funeral pyre. Torch-bearing
gangs of Hindus call to Sikhs to *come out, come out,*
wherever you are. Flames, ignited with flesh, flare
and spread like a bushfire chasing thin stalks of
people across the city. Bodies combust instantly,
that rare phenomenon where people catch fire from
the inside. Flaming coils of cotton, ripped from
knotted heads, dot the streets like stars. The red
moon rises, bearing witness to a flooding tide.

KARMA

Be ready to go

Bapu's parting words. *Be ready.*
I was silent.
We'll take a train if we can.
But for where?
Simla? Kanpur?
Does tolerance live in the hills to the north?
Or to the east?
Will we still go to Chandigarh?
To the relatives who don't speak to each other.
Except at weddings. Mine.

Before he left, Bapu asked for my forgiveness.
It was a mistake to promise me to a man.
A mistake he would correct.
But what if he can't?
And my fate is sealed?
A mother's last wish?
A dowry paid?
Too much shame on the family
for a cancelled bride?

Be ready. Pack your bag. Just one. The smallest.

I push a new *salwar kameez* with scarf to the
bottom of my backpack. One pair of blue
jeans. Two T-shirts. A blouse. Then Mata's
orange sari. (Bapu doesn't know I brought it.)
The zipper won't close when I try to stuff the

diary in too. I know he'll be mad but I throw
the *salwar kameez* to the floor and put on Mata's sari.

I find some rupees under the mattress.
Our passports in the drawer.
And two first-class tickets to Chandigarh.
I lay them all beside Mata's urn on top of the
dresser. Like an offering.

I can't believe he left her behind.

Heat

I lie down on the bed. Wait alone. I am tired of
alone.

Remember, be still. No one should know you are here.

I stare at the ceiling. Dry curls of paint. In stiff
white waves. Like Helen's back after she got
sunburned at Hollow Lake last summer. When
she came back from holidays, I peeled two-inch
strips from her shoulders, thin as parchment.

> (Were her lies already
> forming in new skin?)

I stare at the ceiling fan, stirring air like warm
pudding. *Click. Click.* It counts out time. *Click.
Click.*

> (Is there still time left?
> For Sikhs to escape?
> For Bapu, for me?)

Outside, the city is heavy with humidity and
dread. No wind or breeze ripples. No fresh air
enters the lungs of a country maddened with fury.

India is suffocating.

I hear voices float in from the street below, up to

the fifth-story window of the Rama Hotel. Angry.
Crying. Demanding a victim. Sounds of
vengeance carried on wings. Like the eagle god
Garuda, hider of the moon, destroyer of obstacles
in its way.

(Is Bapu in the way?)

People are dying in New Delhi, he said. And
elsewhere too. Violent, bloody, noisy deaths. Not
like Mata's death. The narrowed airway. The
scarf. The wind. Alone in the afternoon. The
quiet fan.

Out of sight

I had known where to hide after Mata did what
she did. In a field. Under the dry sunflowers.
Face buried in the iron-scented earth. Trying to
forget

her feet
bare
cold
blue
a silver anklet
tinkling in the breeze
an orange sari
circling the neck
a green sari
falling on straw
feet
bare
a naked breast
Mata
Helen
orange sari
green
blue

The wind betrays me

A mauve evening sky pushing a long current of air
across the flat prairie. Ripping through the crops,
dividing the rows, and revealing my hiding place.

I dig my hands into the soil, fingers clenching the
short roots. Hold on, inhale the smell, a scent of
safety, of comfort, of assurance, *love*, but
something pulls at my ankles and rips me from the
dead garden. Seeds fall from above.

I cry out for Mata, but there's no answering voice,
just Bapu's arms dragging me away. Along a trail
of broken stalks.

Leave me here, I cry. I'd rather die.

*You cannot die. It's not what your mother
would have wanted.*

> (But she wanted this?
> That I would find her
> hanging from a ceiling fan?)

A fan. But no *click*. No *whir*.
Because time had stopped.

*Your mother had a dream for your life.
The least we can do now is try to honour it. So, you
cannot die.*

Bapu said this just before he opened
the door to our small kitchen and the
police sitting around the table.

Bapu had known even then what he would do.

We'd be leaving Canada.
For a red sari.

The police

Where were you, Jiva?

In the fields.

Before that?

At a friend's house.

Who?

Helen
(Of Elsinore.)

What were you doing
at Helen's house?

Nothing.

What were you
planning to do?

Nothing.
(Spy on her and
that creep Michael.)

Your father says you come
home every day after school
to be with your mother.
Why not today?

I don't know.

Nothing special about today?

No.

Helen would say it wasn't
special either?

No. She wouldn't say that.

So there was a reason you
were at Helen's today.

Helen wouldn't say that because
she didn't know I was there.

So, you went to see your friend
and she wasn't home.

No. I mean, yes.
She was at home.

Jiva, you're not making any sense.

(No, what doesn't make
sense is when your best
friend steals your clothes,
pretends to be Indian, and
then does it with the boy you
like. And then when you run
home across the fields, your
face wet with tears and
shame, you realize that the
piano is silent. And will be
forever.)

That day

There *were* other days that I didn't come home right
after school. Choir practice. School newspaper.
Some afternoons I even pretended I wasn't there.
Sneaking into the house, quietly climbing to the
second floor-landing. I crouched outside the door,
listening to the sad fingers playing the sad keys.
Her music was different if she didn't think anyone
was listening. Even more heartbreaking.

Sometimes I was caught and Mata became
agitated, even angry. *I was waiting for you*, she said.
Worried about where you were. But we both knew
this wasn't true. My mother had no sense of time
and no sense of motherhood. And in the last few
years had lost her sense of seasons too. I often
found her playing the piano with the window wide
open in the middle of winter. Snow settled along
the sill like white fur.

But we pretended that her anger was real. I kissed
her hands and apologized. She patted my face like
I was a dog.

But that day, I lingered at the highway where the
bus had dropped me. I was trying to decide
whether to cut across the field or take the road. I
hated the fields in the fall. Charred
stubble from the fall burn. In others the sunflower

heads hung like a surrendered army. But that day, I heard Beethoven singing with the wind. The song of loneliness. And despair. Though I didn't know real despair yet, the lesson still to come. But I knew loneliness, the empty river that flowed under my skin and through the blackened earth. That's when I turned for Helen's place. An instinct more than a decision. I wanted to know the truth.

Overheard in Helen's barn

Do I look like her?

Not so much. Does she know you have it?

She said I could borrow it.

I thought the two of you weren't talking.

She lent it to me a long time ago. It's silk, you know.

Are you sure you're wearing it right?

I know. I can't quite get this part right.
The gathering at the front.

It looks different on her. Maybe your hair's too short.
Or too blond. And you don't have the right jewelry
either. Like that sexy nose ring thing.

Okay. Okay. Enough of the comparisons, Michael. I
think it looks good on me. Especially when I dance.

Yes. But honestly, Helen, I don't think it's meant to be
worn with so many clothes underneath.

You're right. It's supposed to be worn with a long slip.

I was thinking maybe with nothing.

Bare skin? I guess I could try that. Now close your eyes.

The Door

We're taught at school:
>If you suspect a fire, feel the door first. If
>it's hot, don't open it. Go to the window
>and yell.

Last month's fire drill. Waiting on the school
sidewalk without jackets. The air cold enough for
snow. Brittle. Knife-edged. *Make a line!* a frantic
teacher shouts. *Orderly now, grade nines!*

But we're too cold to be orderly, Michael says loudly.
He walks down the line of students jumping up and
down to keep warm and points at the breasts of
each girl. *You're cold. You're cold. You're not.*
Hmm. Oh, but you're really cold, Helen of Elsinore.

>(What? How does Michael
>know the secret name?)

I think Jiva's cold too, he says. *Like a lot.* Helen
giggles. I cross my arms. And that's when I
guessed it. Michael *and* Helen.

Dear Maya,
It wasn't your fault. None of it. Not me.
Not Helen. Don't forget this. We own our
lives.

Waves

Get out! Now!

A voice shouts in the hallway.
Waking me.

Hurry!

Fists bang on the door.

Quick! Everyone out!

I feel the hotel door. It's cool to touch but there's
a distinct smell of smoke. I throw back the
curtains and see billowing waves tumbling outside
the window.

Bright flickers of orange ignite in the smoke.
Flames leap across the narrow passageway
between the buildings.
A fire is seeking oxygen.

Get out! Get out!

                                        (Stay hidden. Wait for me.)

Get out! Or be burned!

Yes or no?

There's no time to think.

Hurry! Hurry!

But I'm not ready.

Be ready, Jiva.

The top of the dresser:
passports, rupees, hotel key,
and scissors.
The silver blades.
I pick them up and weigh my options.
My braid.

(Could I be a boy?)

Yes or no?

Get out! Get out!

Yes or no? Yes or no?
Faith. Vanity. What does it matter now?

The braid falls beside Bapu's hair. Already a
forgotten relic. I push at the dark strands with my
foot and recoil. It's like touching dead things.

I strip off my sari and slip, pull on jeans and a T-shirt.

I remove my earrings and nose ring. Rub
the *tikka* from my forehead. I look at my slippers.
I tear at the beads and sequins. Run them under
the tap until they darken.

Hurry!

I slip my feet into wet satin.
Through the open door I see people running down
the hall. *Bapu!* I call out, just in case he has
returned. *Amar! It's Jiva!* Men run by me, but
none is my father. They are all wearing turbans.
Blue. Red. Yellow.

Who or what will save them now? Courage?
God? A sympathetic Hindu?

I hold out the scissors for any who will dare.

It's a trap

A gang carrying sticks waits outside the lobby
doors. They shout: *Indira was our mother and we
will avenge her!* They don't enter the hotel. There's
no need. The guests are trapped. They will either
burn or flee through the narrow doors where the
clubbing will happen. For the young men this is
more efficient. And safer than entering a building
about to catch fire.

I push my way back. Against a crowd unaware
they run from one danger to another. There must
be another exit. A kitchen! Where's the kitchen?

The restaurant is at the back of the hotel. The
doors held closed by two white-jacketed men.
Rectangular towels hang from their arms like
small white flags. Are they are statues or guards
of hell? Why haven't they gone home? Don't
they realize the danger? And besides, who will
come and eat now? The city isn't hungry except
for vengeance.

I bang on the doors, but the waiters lean in. I lift
my backpack and throw it against the door. The
glass holds, but their grip on the handles is
loosened. I push the doors open and run past more
white-jacketed waiters. They watch me but don't
react. Have they seen it all before?

I move along the wall until I find an open window. The drop is far, but it's my only chance. Garbage breaks my fall—cardboard, paper, plastic bottles, food scraps, the sleeping bodies of sick dogs—and then I run. Away from the flames, away from the gangs, away from the cries of broken victims, and into the darkness of the city.

Dear Maya,
Run.

Urn

I forgot Mata.

November 2-3, 1984

Night

I do not sleep.
I listen to my feet.
Running up and down the alleys
of Chandni Chowk.
I do not sleep.
I listen to the city.
The angry animal
feeding its lust and hatred.
I listen to my breath.
The frightened animal
sucking on air.
I do not sleep.
Next to the chai stall
in the dusty hours of night.
But dream.

A dead animal.
Brought back to life
out of darkness.
The body twitching,
the muscles convulsing.
It knows it should run
but instead it waits.
Waits.
For me?
I look up at the face.
And then I see.
It's guarding me.

Watching over me.
Eyes and ears
sharpened for danger.

When I hear the cry
the animal stiffens.
It pokes me in the ribs.
Saying
it's time
poke
wake up now
poke
it's time to run again.

Follow me, the animal instructs.
I know where to go.
I open my eyes.
See the creature bounding
through the narrow streets.
A small deer.
Or an antelope?

Boy!

Chai! Chai now!

Boy! A foot gouges my side. *Get us some chai!*

Boy? I run my hand through my hair. Yes, it's
gone. That part wasn't a dream. I stand slowly.
Touch my backpack to make sure it's still there.
Keep my face hidden until I'm upright, then turn
and run.

They chase me, but I'm faster. Is fear quicker than
anger?

They tire quickly. Their strength used up. How
many times have they raised their arms? Brought
down on innocent heads and backs? How many
like us? Hair short and ragged.

I run. And run.
There's no time to weep. For hair.
Or ashes. Or life.

The station in Old Delhi

Train stations are for journeys.
Departures. Arrivals.

Train stations are for waiting.
Hot. Crowded.

Train stations are for certainty.
Timetables. Clocks.

Train stations are for order.
Uniforms. Guns.

A train station should be safe.

Waiting

I wait through the day.

(Where are you?)

I wait through the night.

(Where?)

Then a morning. A new day.

But still no Bapu. Not on a platform, or in a
ticket line, or in front of the station where the
rickshaws wait and the army stands.

He'd know I'd come here.

(Where else could I go?)

He'd remember the tickets. The day of our
departure. He'd come if he could. Wouldn't
he? He'd realize I was here.

(Wouldn't you?)

More waiting

At noon, the train to Simla departs. Six hours late.
Trains to Lucknow and Kanpur, eight hours. Then
Bombay. Eleven. Varanasi. Cancelled. Who
needs a holy city when there's a holy war?

I watch the half-empty trains arrive. I watch the
swarming trains depart.

A rumour starts that Sikhs have poisoned the
drinking water. Now everyone will want to leave
Delhi and there aren't enough trains.

At seven the sun goes down. And I run out of time.
I force my way to the ticket counter. Shove people
aside. I need a train. Anywhere. Any cost. But
no, not tonight's train to Chandigarh. Can I cash
these tickets in?

I say the word *Canada* to the clerk as if it's a magic
talisman. I put a pile of rupees on the counter. *For
you. Any train. Leaving New Delhi. But not to the Punjab.
I don't want to be on a train with any Sikhs.*

One way. Second Class. Non-AC. Platform 3.

To Jodhpur.

(Wherever that is.)

He'd come if he could. Wouldn't he?

Midnight

The train pulls out at after midnight. *It's late.*
Midnight. *It's early.* Midnight. The passengers
complain. No one is certain which train we are on.
Bombay? Jodhpur? Lucknow, insists one man. *No.*
This train passes through Gurgaon, another says.
Gurgaon? But that's the wrong direction to Lucknow!
And now four people crowd in front of the open
door, staring at the web of tracks passing under
the car.

A man jumps off and calls to his wife. *Jump down!*
We're still in the railyard! There's time to go back and
get on the right train! He runs alongside pleading
with her. *Jump, jump or you will be alone!* he shouts.
No! No! she cries. *I cannot jump!* But suddenly she
is in the air, falling. Not making a sound.

I think she was pushed.

Dark

They climb in the dark like river rats onto a barge.
Hands and feet scrambling up the barred windows.
Footsteps drumming on the metal roof. Their
voices shout when they reach the top. But not all
make it. Bodies fall past the window.

Are they Sikhs escaping?
Hindus pushing them off?
Or is it only the poor traveling for free?

The conductor enters the car to punch our tickets.

Are we are going to Jodhpur?

Most likely, he says. *But who can know in these
times?*

I hear the rumour again. How a train from Punjab
pulled into the station. Massacred Hindus spilled
out in a river of blood.

I didn't see any blood. All day.

Lock the door. Don't open it for anyone.

Yes. Gangs of angry men can't get into a locked
train.

Overheard in the night

- *There's nothing to be afraid of anymore.*

- *The further we get from Delhi, the better.*

- *Delhi is the craziest city, always out of control about something.*

- *Well, this isn't just something.*

- *I don't understand why they did it. Those bodyguards. Sikhs have always been the protectors of Hindus.*

- *But remember what she did to the Golden Temple.*

- *I was brought up believing that Sikhs were the proudest, most courageous people of all Indians.*

- *But aren't Sikhs really just Hindus who made up a religion?*

- *Yes. But in some ways all religions are made up.*

- *Well, I don't understand what's happening. I have Sikhs who are friends. But maybe I don't know anything about them.*

- *Well try understanding this! It was a Hindu servant who marked my door with charcoal. So the mob knew which house to incinerate!*

Dear Maya,
You were right to save yourself.

White gloves

The rocking of the train puts me to sleep.

In the dream a uniformed man is directing traffic.
He stands on a dais in the middle of a crowded
street. Taxis, rickshaws, motorcycles, bicycles go
round and round like a giant traffic circle without
an exit.

At first, he uses his white gloves to orchestrate the
traffic, but no one is paying him any attention. The
cars circle until they become stuck. People are
shouting at each other in anger, but no one can
move.

The traffic policeman unwraps his turban and
whips it at the cars. The direction of the cloth tells
the drivers which way to go. The drivers are
shouting because it is too confusing. No one can
move. The man is unperturbed.

He continues to spin the cloth; it floats, ripples in
the bright air, a ribbon of intention, a ribbon of
thought coming from his own mind, and then I see,
for the first time, that it's not a policeman, it's the
prime minister. She's directing traffic. She's the
one not listening to the drivers. And now the cloth
is a whip coming down on their heads.

At first the people cower, are brought to their knees as they ward off the blows, but still the traffic is not moving, so their anger grows. They want to move. They are tired of being stuck in this circle. One man stands up to her and his bravery spreads. They rush at her, knocking her from her platform in the centre of the road. Their hands pull her body apart.

The night should have ended

We sigh when the sun rises. Another day further
from the madness.

The Hindus face the morning rays and chant,
palms together, heads bowing, beads in hand.

A Muslim man spreads out his prayer mat and
kneels. The train changes direction and he turns
too. To Mecca.

When the Sikh man speaks I know the words.
My father's voice in the early light. The sun has
risen every day of my life with this song.
Is it possible Bapu is reciting this prayer? In a
quiet place, where it's safe to call out his faith? Or
perhaps he hides? And dares not breathe? Or
make a sound to save his life? Perhaps he
searches for me now in the burned skeleton of the
Rama Hotel. Or waits on Platform 3.

A woman pulls sections from a guava and passes
them around the car. Juice rolls down our faces
while the steel wheels spin. We are at peace.
Hindus, Muslims, and a Sikh. A Canadian girl of a
mixed-religion. Dressed as a boy.

When the sun rises, is it always a new day?

Where?

He'd have come if he could. Wouldn't he?

Naked

A naked child pees on the floor. A shimmering
little pool. She leans down to touch it.

When the train makes a turn, a thin yellow
tributary separates and runs towards the door.
The child laughs.

But when I smell the sour urine I only smell
fear.

I pull my scarf over my mouth and nose.
Take short breaths.
    In out
    in out
    breathe through the mouth
    don't smell

The child pees some more. But this time cries.

The wheels grind. Spark.
And brake.

Mirage

They come across the yellow fields
running with dark faces and teeth bared
through ribbons of heated air
a mirage of false water.

The train slows as if waiting for them to catch up.

What's happening?
Why are we stopping here?
Is it wolves?

But they are not wolves

                                (we should have prayed for wolves)

but men instead
four-limbed and angry
carrying iron rods and knives
hands gripping gasoline cans
voices shouting into the hot dry air
their fury stirring the dust like a wind.

                                (we should have prayed for wolves)

They slam their bodies against the slowing
train. They cling to the window bars. They
climb to the roof and throw people into the air.
A voice demands we unlock the door of our
carriage. *Open or be burned!*

I tell myself I'm still sleeping:
the unwound turban meting out

punishment
a gang of men severing the body of the
    prime minister
the pounding of their fists
    on this train
    on this car
are only hammering
the metal walls of my head.

Open or be burned!

We must save ourselves! someone cries.

But it is no dream
    my hands and arms know
    my nostrils know
    even my lungs and
    my shallow breaths
    know
    what my heart cannot fathom
    know
    what's going to happen next
    because in dreams you cannot close
    your eyes and mine are shut tight.

We must save ourselves!

The door opens.

Oh my God. Who unlocked the door?

No!

Leave him! I shout.
What are you doing?
Leave him!
Leave him alone!
He's done nothing!
It wasn't him who killed the prime minister!
Don't take him!
You have no right!

The Sikh man clings to me as if I'm a pole or a
mast and a sea is rising all around us. I try
to hold him in my arms. Dig my fingers into
his flesh like hooks, but the men pull at him
while hitting me. I grab for the thigh, the knee,
the foot that shakes with terror, and I am left
with a shoe. A black leather shoe with the
narrow lace tied neatly into a bow. Its
emptiness horrifies me. The dark cavern where
the foot had been. Where the foot . . . .

Please don't take him.
He could be your brother.
Your uncle.
Your father.

He could be all you have left in this world.

Man as child

They bind his legs with the long cotton of his
turban. His dark knotted hair revealed to God
—his reverence, protection of the self, now
unwound. He is a child without the turban,
crying in terror as the gasoline cools his sweat
like ice.

The match catches fast. A magic trick.
Flesh conjuring the wind. Sweeping across the
yellow field, turning the man into a pillar of
fire.

His scream splits my chest open.
But I can't move.
I am held down by my horror.

The Sikh grows in his death.
Only a man and yet such a blaze.
Made of spirit and bone.

He grows in his death
larger than anyone
could imagine.
Transformed
into a dragon
without a body.

And he is nameless.

Don't breathe

I stuff my scarf
over my nose
stuff it in my mouth
swallow it
hold myself down
don't breathe
don't breathe
if I don't breathe
I won't smell
I won't smell
I won't smell
    the reek of murder

No whistle

The train pulls away before the flames die.
No whistle is needed.
The women wail.
I wail.
A funeral hymn.

The Sikh was large in his death.
We were small in our cowardice.
We should be mourning for our own lost souls.

We didn't do enough.
We didn't do anything at all.

Dear Maya,
Not everyone can be saved.

The journey should have ended

Hours ago, days. Months. An epoch. The
passengers have aged beyond recognition, creased
faces, shaking hands holding stomachs, heads,
children, and the sun won't set and give us peace—
it's tethered to the train like a hot balloon, dragged
through a bleached sky.

The train inches its way across the tired land, the
wheels pushing through ash, cutting through
scorched limbs. Small fires smoulder, marking the
route. Other trains have been this way, stopped
by wolves (if only it had been wolves) in the
middle of nowhere.

The black line of track scores the wounded earth.
Like a cracked heart.

My question

Who opened the door?
Would the lock not have held?

They look away, but I keep asking:
Who let them in?
Was it you?
Or you? Who?
Which one of you?

> *- It doesn't matter.*
> *-They would have come anyway.*
> *- They would have killed all of us.*
> *- Did you not see their faces?*
> *- And the cans of petrol?*

Then we all should have died.
We deserved to die if we didn't
try to save him.

> *- Maybe it was you.*

What?

> *- Maybe it was you who opened the door.*
> *- Yes. It was. I saw.*
> *- It was him.*
> *- The strange boy. Him.*
> *- Yes, I saw it too.*
> *- It was you who opened the door.*
> *- We saw.*
> *- We all saw.*
> *- It was you.*
> *- Why did you open the door?*
> *- Who are you?*

The guilty one

Even the peeing girl points to me.

It was you.

I want to hit them.
Send them flying across the car.

Can't they see what's happening?
How our guilt turns to rage?
How it burns in our muscles?
How blame is the only salve?

I shout at them to look away.

Leave me alone!

But they can't.
They stare in accusation.
Like me, they are rooted at
this moment in time where
fear makes black eyes unblinking,
and skin burns like paper.

It was you who opened the door.

Is Delhi burning?

Tell us. Quick.

The train slows in the Jodhpur station
and already the voices are clamouring for news.

Is New Delhi burning? How many dead?

Those who've been waiting for eleven hours throw
themselves against the hot metal like lizards in the
sun. They peer through the bars. Arms, eyes,
hearts searching. For relatives. For arms, eyes,
hearts that might be missing.

Where is he?

They pound the cars.

Where is Simar? Where is Navjeet?
Where is Ravinder?

They force their way onto the train.

Where is Hardeep?

They search the faces of those who remain.

What have you done with them?

The train is only two-thirds full.

What? Set on fire?

The wailing begins again. They cannot be calmed.
A single note of the deepest sorrow.

aiiiiiiiiiiiiiiiiii

I slither onto the platform, lean into the pulsing
mass of torsos and heads. I push against the dark
crowd, but they push back, their limbs tangled with
mine. My muscles burn, but I cannot get free. I
feel my flesh tighten over bone. Fuse to my rage.

Where were you?

It was you.

Knives of heat pierce the white air.

Mata and Bapu were wrong

I am not *life*.
I am not *illusion*.
I am the *Goddess of Death*.

I open my eyes into the hot rays of sunlight
and let them catch fire. Then I turn my gaze
to the crowd with a burning hatred.

I mix up my words. And my languages. Hindi and
Punjabi and English are stirred into an angry
tongue. I am the embodiment of the painful history
of this country.

It wouldn't take much.
To rip you open.
Your thin rippled chests
crumpling under my fists.
I could reach into the
pits of your desperate bellies
and pull out your livers.
Watch me.
Watch me meet your rage with mine.
Watch me set you on fire with my vengeance.

I swing my arms and feel flesh against my
knuckles. A small inch of space opens and I swing
again. A man sputters and steps back. Another
punch. A cheekbone this time. More space. Now
there's room for my legs to move. I kick at anyone

who's near me, striking them like chickens until
they half fly away and a path opens up before me.

They will not fight me. They will let me go. But
my will collapses.

I stand in the silenced crowd and suddenly cannot
move. I am unable to take a step from the women
and men who will soon find out that their husbands
and fathers and brothers and sons have been left in
a field. Smouldering.

I fall. Headfirst into the wide gap I've carved with
my rage. When my knees hit the ground, the
crowd closes over me like a healing wound.

I cannot breathe under the stomping legs and am
glad for it. Soon I will no longer smell the scent of
death. Except my own.

November 4, 1984

Voices

- *Is it a girl?*

- *I don't know. Look at the hair.*

- *A widow then, like us?*

- *Can't be. Look at the clothes.*

- *Maybe a* farange? *From England?*

- *But the skin is dark like ours.*

- *Then an Indian. A boy.*

- *But so pretty. Like a* kothi.

$\mathcal{M}$usic

Are you all right?

Words sing in my ear.

Are you all right?

A cool voice. A breeze. Sliding in from a far-off
ocean, not a land voice. Words softly spoken but
sharply enunciated. A woman.

Are you all right?

All right. All right. Hum. Hum. I try to sing along.

The woman's face is thrown into shadow by a
bright light hovering behind her head. But I can
make out a black braid, draped over the shoulder.
And a blue sari and a dark leather bag by her side.

I am Dr. Parvati Patel. What's your name?

When she leans over me, I hear the sound of ice
tinkling against glass. Golden bracelets circling the
small wrists.

And then I remember.
The man's arms had been thin and brown too. But
swollen blue veins were their only adornment.

I am glad you're awake.

Her hand touches my forehead. I hear myself groan. Like an animal in pain.

You have a fever.

A fever? I consider the word, but it seems so mild a term for the heat that burns under my skin. I place the back of my hand on my face.

(Do I have a mother
who does this?)

And then I remember.
No. It's not just a fever. I take a deep breath.
My chest aches as if something has been pulled out
from under the ribs.

*I know what happened on the train. And at the
station.*

The woman's small lips are pulled tight across her face. Creased dark brown circles ring her eyes.

*You collapsed and were brought here. No one will claim
you.*

My eyes look past her. A narrow doorway leads

to the outside. Strips of sunlight flash like flames
as a curtain lifts and falls with a breeze.

*Can you tell me who you are? Can you tell me
anything? Please. I'm a doctor. I want to help.*

The curtain shudders. The wind rises and then is
gone. My voice lashed to it.

Not Indian

Someone said that you're not Indian.

                                        (No, I am dead.)

The doctor crouches down to face me directly.
Now I can see her face. Her large dark irises and
long lashes hide almost all the whiteness of her
eyes.

Where are you from?

                                        (From hell.)

But I answer, *J'habite à Elsinore. Je suis
étudiante.* Madame Kirby's practiced phrases fall
from my mouth. I must be in hell. I am speaking
French.

The doctor looks puzzled. Her long elegant nose
wrinkles. Then her upper lip, plum-shaded and
stained the colour of wine, curls over the lower.
I must be babbling.

Can you tell me your name? she asks again in Hindi.

Name? A French name? A dead name? But the
word forms in my mouth like a bubble. *Maya,*
pops out.

Maya. Lovely. I'm sorry, Maya, for what you've seen.

Her hand touches my forehead again. The
bracelets ringing like bells.

*Did you know that Mrs. Gandhi's death was predicted
by many wise men? Some say even Mrs. Gandhi knew
what was to come.*

Are you a goddess? I want to ask her. Her skin is
so perfect. Creamy not brown. Unflawed and
unlined. Are you Saraswati?

*How can one protect oneself from Fate? It flies out
of the darkness, beating its wings, and carries away our
souls.*

She talks like a goddess.

*Don't worry, Maya. In time the world will come to its
senses.*

She stands up. Her sari rustling like autumn
leaves. She seems to float above me, a brightly
coloured peacock lifting into air.

When she ducks under the doorway, the curtain
follows her like a shadow. *I'll be back soon.*

People are being burned alive. My parched lips blow
out the words. *Burned alive,* I whisper, for the last
time.

uilt

I know I'm not the one who
unwrapped the turban, bound
the legs, poured the gasoline,
and struck the match.

(And I'm not the one who
wrapped the orange sari
around her neck.)

But I listened to the screams
for mercy and was frozen.

(I hid behind the barn door
and watched Michael
undress Helen.)

Could I have smothered the
fire with my body?

(What if I'd gone home
right after school?)

Should I have died with him?
Fire on my hands?

(I could have followed my
father. Not left him alone.)

Is my silence unfounded too?

No. I do not deserve to be found.
Or loved.

Please talk to me, the doctor begs. *Where's your
mother, your father, your family? Let me help you.
Someone needs to know where you are.*

And sometimes there's nothing left
to say to another human being.

Dear Maya,
Forget what you've seen. Let the heart go.
Just sleep. A dream doesn't mean it's not
real.

Sandeep's Notebook

November 13, 1984

Top six reasons to (maybe) keep a diary

#1. YOU'RE ALWAYS RIGHT In the middle of an
argument with a family member who doubts your
memory of events, you can whip out the diary and set
them straight.

#2. GIRLFRIEND When your girlfriend wants to
know where you've been or what you've been doing,
you can find the right date and prove your
whereabouts. Undeniable facts!

#3. LIES Fill your diary with lies and you can
actually rewrite history and challenge everyone's
memory. That's kind of cool.

Okay. That's the same reason as #2.
And #1.

#4. LIFE-CHANGING EVENT When something big
is on the horizon (you recognize this by the tremours in
the pit of your stomach), you can write down
everything that's happening and go back later to
figure out: WHY ME?

#5. THE LOST GIRL Something's going on there. You
don't get it. (Nobody does.) But one day it may all make
sense and you could have the pieces to the puzzle.

Oh, great. Now #4 and #5 are the same.

#6. PARVATI When your sister asks you for a favour, you do it.

Top three reasons to (maybe) keep a diary

#1. Lies

#2. Truth

#3. Duty

Top reason to not keep a diary

What if someone reads it?

(And they realize you're just an idiot.)

Duty

You know, for most people, a diary's just
a ribbon of random thoughts vaguely
linked by grammatical laws and scribbled
across a page when there's nothing better
to do.
I mean: why describe life when you can
just get out there and LIVE it?
I'd rather do trigonometry.
Tangents bold as horizon lines.
Circles divided evenly by π.
SINE: Elegantly connected triangular
relationships. (From the Sanskrit word
jiva, Mr. Banerjee explained.)

But girls? They love this shit. Pouring out
their innermost thoughts and feelings!
Thick as syrup! And honestly, how much
is there really to think about? How much
is there really to *feel?*

I read Parvati's diary once.
It was full of DESPAIR.
HOPELESSNESS.
(For the poor and sick.)
And not one mention of LOVE.
Still, it managed to be sentimental (maybe
girls can't help it!) even though she's the
smart one in the family. The DOCTOR.

According to Amma (my adoptive mother), my
sister's education has almost lifted our
family up a caste to where it should be (if it
wasn't for me).
Not that Barindra-Pita (adoptive father) gives a
rat's ass about social ranking.
Because, you see, I'm the one responsible
for our humble stature.
'Cause I'm the ORPHAN.
THE DIAMOND IN THE ROUGH.
(At least, this is what Barindra told Amma
when he brought me home.)
I am the Patels' *GOOD DEED*.
The adopted child who improves
the family karma.

In reality, I'm a shepherd's son.
Found under a goat.
My parents dead.
Drowned in sand.
And yeah, that's a bit sad.
Girls like it though.
They get all teary-eyed when
I tell them the story.
And then they let me kiss them.

But here's the thing:
I'M NOT THE KIND OF
GUY WHO KEEPS A DIARY
Words are for talking.
Words are for bartering.

Words are for seducing.
Chandi. Priti. Tejal.
Words are for getting what you want.
Words are not for putting in a book
where somebody might find them.

I mean have you ever heard of a
seventeen-year-old boy doing such
a thing?

But here I am.
Writing.
Because after what Parvati
did for me, I can't say no.

Dear Diary

Nah. That's lame.
(Be creative, you idiot!)

DEAR LOST GIRL
Who are you?
Whence have you come?
Will you tell me your secrets, o voiceless one?
O yuck.

DEAR GIRL-WITH-GODDESS NAME
If illusion be your given name
and mystery wears your opaque veil
then I, Sandeep, with pen as sword
will scribe your silence
till you are *cured.*
(or till I'm bored)
(till I'm adored?)
(till I am gored)
(or deplored)
(or suitably and deservedly well ignored)

Rhyming diphthongs. How pathetic.

Oh, another thing

Parvati thinks I should write in English!

> - *It'll be good practice. You've been out of*
> *school for a year now. And if Mother finds*
> *your notebook she won't be able to read it!*

So here goes. Hope Lost-Girl doesn't mind.
(Not that I intend to tell her. Because it's a
pretty weird thing to do. Write about someone
who has sealed their own tongue.)

DEAR MAYA
My sister insists I keep a record of the comings
and goings of a troubled mute girl. YOU. (WHO,
by the way, I haven't met yet.)

I am to be your voice until your own returns.
This is what Parvati says. (*It's simple, Sandeep.*)
A little pompously?

Oh, and no offense, Maya, but when has silence
ever helped anybody?

I think Gandhi said something like that.

Added bonus

Parvati thinks this diary is a good way to dig
up some history. Mine. My former desert life. Swept
from memory by a once-in-a-century sandstorm.

But here's the thing: maybe some things are supposed
to stay in the past. I mean, doesn't the PAST mean
it's OVER?

Pavarti

It's my sister's fault. How this whole thing
started. Her phone call from Jodhpur that
caused our mother to run screaming and
hobbling down the street with Barindra in
pursuit.

> *- And why should I keep a notebook, Deedi? You
> know nothing ever happens in Jaisalmer.*

> *- Well, something is about to, brother. As I
> just told Amma, I'm sending a girl.*

Okay. I was a little hooked.

> *- Sandeep? Can you hear me?*

> *- Yes. Yes. Are you crazy, Deedi? What kind
> of girl? Better not be a bride for me!*

Laugh. Laugh.

> *- Not a bride, Sandeep. It's a girl who was
> dropped off at the Widows' Home in Jodhpur.*

Uh, oh.

> *- A child widow? Or a child prostitute?
> Because either way Amma won't have her
> in the house. No matter what Barindra says.*

- She's neither. I think she's a foreigner
  escaping the riots in Delhi. The girl tried to
  disguise herself. Though I think she's far too
  pretty to be mistaken for a boy.

Hook sliding under the skin.

  - How old?

  - I'm guessing she's about your age.

SUPER-hooked.

  - Her name is Maya, Sandeep.

My stomach flipped. Just like the time I
jumped across a broken parapet on a dare.
I was either going to make it and be seen as
incredibly brave or I would fall, break my neck,
and be viewed as a fool.

  - Sandeep? Are you still there?

Maya. My heart beat like a desert drum. Palms
dripping sweat.

  - Yes, I'm here.

  - She came to us wearing blue jeans and a
  T-shirt with English words: Triumph on the

front. Never Surrender *on the back.*

Now, I don't believe in fate.

> *- And her hair is very short. Looks like it was cut quickly and badly. Maybe with a pair of dull scissors.*

And I don't believe in destiny.

> *- Did I mention, Sandeep, that she doesn't speak? Can't or won't, I'm not sure. But the girl is clearly traumatized. And that's where you come in.*

But I was already in. My body was shuddering as if it knew. Something big was about to happen in this dull desert town. And I'd be in the middle of it. With a girl named Maya.

Sing

My sister has a theory about me:
You can make a stone sing, Sandeep.

What she means is that people tell me stuff.
    (The butcher in the market
    substitutes dog meat for lamb.)

Private things. Secrets.
    (Hari enjoys dressing in his sister's clothes.)

You have a gift, Parvati says. *People want to reveal
themselves to you.*
    (Tejal aces her math tests by allowing
    Mr. Banerjee to touch her breasts —
    though she won't let me!)

There's no trick to it really. Just listen. Not judge.
Once people feel safe it's rather incredible to watch.
They lean in. Whisper in your ear. Sometimes they
even cry as they confess their lie or small crime.
    (Our neighbour Mr. Gupta is in love
    with his wife's sister. They meet in
    secret and he recites poetry to her.
    It's possible her third child is his.)

*I think if anyone can get Maya to speak, it'll be you,
Sandeep. She won't be able to resist your charms.*

Or my good looks, I answer.

Laugh. Laugh.

It's no secret that I'm not handsome. In the last year
my arms have grown faster than my legs. The hair on
my head won't lie flat no matter how much oil I put
on it. My lips are too full. My ears flap when there's
a wind. I've been likened to a goat. Even Amma
described me as such when Barindra brought me
home from the desert. I was only six years old when
I heard her whisper she'd never seen such an ugly
child. Did I have a tail too?

Maya won't be able to resist your voice, brother.

Patience. Patience is everything. If you're not willing
to wait, the secret keeper will never tell.

Not another orphan!

Amma hates her already.
When she first heard the name *Maya*
her stomach flipped like mine but she
threw up all over the floor.
Yellow *aloo bharta.*
Green *moong dhal.*
Soft chunks of unchewed *roti.*

*See what you've done, Barindra! I have wasted an
entire meal on that girl. And I may never be able to
eat again!*

Amma is high-strung and sensitive. It's her higher
birth, Parvati explained. Born as a Kshatriyas but
had to marry into Barindra's lower Vaishyas caste
when the match-maker couldn't find a man who
didn't mind her limp.

My arrival from a lowly nomadic tribe hasn't
helped the downward slide of her social standing.
And Barindra's bleeding-heart sensibilities only
makes things worse.

She might be a prostitute! Amma cries. *What will
the neighbours say?*

They will say we are kind and generous, Barindra
answers. *Mina, We took in Sandeep when he needed a
home, and now we will take in this girl.*

I don't know why we are the only family who is so committed to saving orphans. How many did Gandhi adopt? None.

Well, perhaps he should have. His own children resented him terribly. Besides, Mina, it's just for a time. Until we find her family. And it's the right thing to do, Barindra insists. You'll see.

What I will see is this family spiral downward. Soon we will have no caste at all and have to clean the toilets!

When she storms off, Barindra takes me aside. *Don't worry, Sandeep. Families aren't supposed to be peaceful. Good families are like steel. Stronger when heated. Then they can withstand anything.*

Well, if this keeps up, the house could go up in flames while we're sleeping and none of us would have a blister.

This is how we heard about Maya

Every Saturday afternoon I squeeze into
a post office telephone booth with Amma
and Barindra. It's the weekly call with Parvati. We
exchange news. Amma scolds. Barindra thanks her
for the money she sends for Amma's Ayurvedic
doctor. (He rubs sand on her leg for ten rupees a
visit!)

I've grown accustomed to the glass door steaming
with communal onion sweat. Our bodies curled,
sticking to each other like soft brown turds nestled in
the pipe of a toilet.
(Nice image. Maybe I am a writer!)

I must wait my turn to talk to Parvati (*No, not outside
the booth!* insists Amma) while enduring the scent of
curry breath yellowing the air with questions:
- *How is the temperature of Jodhpur, Parvati? Ah!*
  Same as here.
- *What is the price of rice? Chicken? Bananas? Aiii!*
  You pay too much! You must haggle like Sandeep to
  get a good price!
- *Have you bought yourself a new sari instead of giving*
  your money to the ungrateful poor?
  Did you hear that cousin Sunita will marry in the
  spring? And she is five years younger than you!

But last Saturday, the conversation didn't wind
through the same old subjects and predictable rants.

My sister jumped right to Maya. Denying her mother
the pleasure of the weekly gossip.

> - *Throw the stubborn girl out on the street,*
>   *Parvati! She'll find her tongue quick enough.*

> - *But Amma, if she's not Indian, she'll never*
>   *survive. No, we must try to help her. Put*
>   *Pita on the phone.*

That's when Amma forced the door open, releasing a
cloud of pungent angry vapor.
(A genie escaping a bottle?) She wept
and screamed openly on the post office floor. Amma
had realized that when Barindra heard the girl's
plight, he would be compelled to offer aid.

Mina, I cannot hear Parvati if you make so much
noise! Barindra shouted through the glass.

So Amma picked herself up and went home. She
waited until we walked through the door before
saying, *Who names a child Maya?*

And then Amma barfed.

One who lights the way

Parvati gave me the name, Sandeep. (She had to,
she said. After the storm, I didn't remember anything.)

She was just sixteen when she reached under the
cooling bellies of a collapsed herd of black and
white goats. She thought they were only skins.

She had heard a cry. A faint bleat. A kid? But there was
a child's foot. Where there shouldn't have been a foot.

How many hours? A day or more did I sleep
under the goats' protection? No one knows.
There was no one left alive to tell.

What I remember is being lifted out of a darkness
damp and soft, then held against a beating heart.
A breath on my face blew the grains of sand from
my crusted eyelids. A goddess smiled down me.
The face of love.

(Oh shit. Now *I'm* writing sentimental crap.)

Years later, Parvati confessed that when our eyes
locked, she knew what she would do with her life.
There's no better joy, Sandeep, than knowing
you've saved a life.

Usually when I get to this part of the story,
some girl is letting my hands wander.

A son

It was Barindra who carried me in. *I have a son,
Mina!* he exclaimed. Amma broke down in tears.
Parvati said she actually pulled her hair out in rage.

She blamed the matchmaker (now dead). *That witch
waited too long to find me a husband so all I could
get was you! And now you bring me this orphan!*

Parvati heard Amma was lucky to have a marriage
match at all. As eldest, she should have married first,
but good matches for her two younger sisters had
come quickly. Eventually, Amma was betrothed to
her middle sister's husband's brother. Ten years
younger. But the dowry was doubled. (Allowing
Barindra to complete his teacher training.)

In spite of the differences in caste, age, temperament
(and one leg shorter than the other), the marriage was
a good one. Barindra let his wife lead him around by
the nose. A child was born to them: the excellent
daughter, Parvati.

But when I arrived (the dusty goat child), Amma
knew things would change if she couldn't produce
her own son. The house rocked for months with the
hopes of conception. (Barindra was pleased with this
new longing in Mina.) But the noisy sex yielded no
new life, so Amma announced her childbearing years
were over and reluctantly cared for me.

Parvati has always said that I was a child who brought happiness and resignation to this family. *But what child doesn't, Sandeep?*

Be yourself

Parvati phoned last night.

 - *When you see Maya, just be you,* she says.

 - *What does that mean?*

 - *Be natural.*

 - *I'm not natural?*

 - *I mean don't fuss over her. Don't treat her
   like she's ill or special or strange. Just, you
   know, be yourself.*

Parvati's the only one who thinks *being myself* is
a good thing.

Amma thinks I don't need any reminding.
I am too much *myself,* and that's my flaw.
She's ready to have me dropped off in the
middle of the desert so I can be *myself* in the
landscape of my lower birth. *Let him go back
to his roots. To his proper destiny,* she tried to
convince Barindra.

But Barindra thinks otherwise. *Don't be yourself,* he
urges me. *Be better! Reach beyond your birthright!
The world is your oyster!* (A bivalve mollusk trapped
in a shell?) *Carve your path but not in sand,*

Sandeep! Sculpt it into something that won't blow away. An education!

Somehow, Barindra's belief in me is even worse than Amma's assessment. He seems to think that my casteless tribal status is not a deterrent in becoming successful. *Gandhi changed this country so a boy like you could rise up!*

Amma is more realistic. *A senior secondary school diploma would be a remarkable achievement.* (But the world won't let you go any higher.) She didn't have to say it out loud.

Parvati believes I should choose my path. *Be whatever you want to be, Sandeep, but at least be the best.*

So I'm a guide now. Lighting the way for tourists who want to explore a city where Sheh'rzaday could have told her tales! The most eloquent tout in all of Jaisalmer! And I give HALF my earnings to my parents. So no one can say I'm not a good son, even if I'm adopted and ugly. And a drop out.

Shrine

Amma is on her knees. Her head bowed to the silver
images. Ganesh and Krishna. Two ghee lamps burn
bright yellow. Jasmine flowers wilt on the pedestal. I
tiptoe past, but she sees me with the eyes in the back
of her head and stops her devotion.

Sandeep?

                                              Yes, Amma.

Do you ever wonder what
I pray for?

                                                    No.

Never?

                                    It is none of my concern.

Hmm. But you must wonder a
little. You're a curious boy. At
some point in the last eleven
years you must have wondered.

I say nothing. A technique learned from Barindra.
The less you say, the less you can
be accused of.

Well?

                                    You have a secret life,
                                    Amma. I respect that.

Hmm. I hope you don't have a
secret life, Sandeep.

                                    No. Never. I have no desire
                                    to prostrate before a god.

That is not what I meant! I
meant . . . oh, never mind.
Sandeep, are you not afraid for
your soul? That it may wander
this earth for a thousand lives?

No, Amma. You and I both
know I'll return to the desert
one day. Perhaps my soul
waits for me there.

Hmm. Like the secretive fox. A
reminder, Sandeep? You're not
to touch.

Touch what?

You're not to touch the girl.
Parvati's orphan. Even if she's
already been touched. Do you
understand?

Perfectly.

All right. You will go to the train
station in the morning. The Jodhpur
Express arrives at nine. I do not want
to be seen in public with her. And
thank God, Barindra will be at the
school. So that leaves you. Bring her
quick. Straight here. Understand?

Yes, Amma. I
understand perfectly.

Awake

I cannot sleep.

Amma and Bahrindra are making their night noises.
Old Dadima too. She snores like her son and daughter-
in-law. Three trains rumbling into the station.

I've heard that in some countries, families sleep apart.
Siblings in their own rooms. Parents separate.
Imagine the peace. No startling cries from your
mother's bad dream. No waking up to find a sister's
braid tickling your face like a rat's tail.

But with walls between the sleeping bodies
there wouldn't be whispers to overhear.

A strange girl of unknown origins? A mute with that
name? That name! It's a bad omen, Barindra!
What were you and Parvati thinking?

What were we thinking? We are Hindu. The girl
may be Sikh. There is a debt to pay.

That is not the name of a Sikh girl! And besides, we
didn't have anything to do with what happened in
Delhi, Barindra. It is not our fault!

Yet by not helping the victims, we are just as guilty.
And forget the name, Mina. It's common enough.

Barindra, I've listened to that name shouted in my home every night for the last eleven years. And you think it's just coincidence!

In the dream

She walks out of the desert wearing a golden sari.
Her hair is long, to her waist, blowing in the wind.
In her hand she holds a pink shell.
She puts it to her mouth and makes a sound.

It sings my name across the sand.

Maya, I call to her.

It's what I always shout when I have this dream.

November 14–21, 1984

Train station

Shit.

Don't be late, Sandeep, Parvati insisted.
She might run.

Run? To where? There's nothing but
desert and Pakistan west of here.
And who wants to go to Pakistan?

But shit. I am late.
I take the steps two at a time.
Dodging porters balancing
suitcases on their heads.
Squeezing between a family
walking seven across like a
line of protesters.

Slow down, you little asshole!
a man shouts after I leapfrog
off his smallest child's head.

Sorry! Thank you! I call over my
shoulder. Amma insists I be
deferential. (*You're a shepherd
boy, after all.*)

Now where would she be in this dung-odoured,
sweat-stained sea of questionable humanity?

Maya hates crowds Parvati said. Kicks at
people if they get too close. Well, good for
her. Some people deserve a good kicking.

I run through the carriages. Third class
smells like piss. Second class like wet goat.
(Strangely comforting.) An AC sleeper? Would
Parvati be so extravagant?

I swing open the doors of
every compartment.
Empty.
Empty.
Empty.
And then I see her.
Blue jeans. T-shirt.
Huddled next to a window.
A bag on her lap.
A face still as stone.

It's just a girl, I tell myself.
(Disguised as a boy.)
I'm good with girls.
But my stomach lurches.
And my heart rate is definitely increasing.
(Even skipping.)

Her face is perfect.
A long slender nose.
Soft curled eyelashes.

Skin polished like dark wood.
She is named well. Goddess of Illusion.

Maya looks like a statue.

Listening

Hello, Maya.

Silence.

I am Sandeep. (Smile.) *Parvati's brother?*

Silence.

I am very pleased to meet you. (Deep bow.)

Kuch nahin! (Not even a flicker of an eyelash.)

I am deeply honoured to come to your aid, Maya.
Honoured indeed to accompany you to the humble home
of the Patel family. (That should do it.)

She turns toward me. Her gaze settles on my face.
There is no expression, no emotion. Yet when her
dark eyes find mine, I am suddenly dizzy. Like I'm
slipping under a black wave soft as silk.

I have never seen, never known such sadness.

Where is my voice?

Chai! Chai!

The repeated staccato sound bursts
into the car like automatic gunfire.

Chai! Chai! Chai! Chai!

An apparition in the shape of a small boy appears
holding a clay cup in two hands.

Chai?

Not waiting for an answer, he pours mud-coloured
liquid from a dented metal pot.
I raise my hand to stop him, but Maya is quicker.
She hits the boy's arm without blinking. Tea
spills across his chest.

Aiii aiii hot chai hot chai!

IT wasN'T thaT hOT! I shout. (Why is my voice
cracking like a twelve-year-old's?) *Get out of
HEre! NoW! NOw!*

The boy lands a sharp kick to my shin, then runs.
ShIT! My leg throbs. A hammer against bone.

I hop up and down to shake off the pain. *We
should go now, Maya,* I whisper.

But she's already moving. Backpack in hand.
Sliding down the narrow hallway.

(*Why did Parvati send an idiot boy for me?*)

What? Did she just say that?
Great. Now my ears aren't working either.

Smoke

Ushering Maya through the train station is like directing smoke. *This way. Left. Here. No. Not there. Over here. Yes. Just follow me. But stay close.*

Don't touch her, Amma had said. She meant SEX, of course, but even tapping Maya on the arm to guide her along the crowded platform seems questionable. If I reach for her will she run? Or dissipate?

People are stepping back to let Maya pass. I hear the voices whisper. *Who's that? You mean what's that?* Someone laughs.

She's as tall as a man. Her hair sticks up in ragged spikes. Her thin body could be a boy's, but the face is definitely a woman's. A mouth that curves up in spite of the sadness.

Is it a he or a she?

Maya doesn't flinch. She ignores them utterly.

It's a kothi. A pretty boy!

No! Here in Jaisalmer?

And this is what Amma was afraid of: the gossips have begun their work.

Hot sun

She refuses to get into a rickshaw. Marches past the
long line of arm-waving, shouting drivers. Ignores
their whining voices.
But why no rickshaw?

She swings her backpack over her shoulder
and walks quickly.

*But it's too far, I say. Really it is. The sun's climbing.
We'll be pools of sweat if we walk.*

She turns onto the main road.

*Okay, so you've found the road. Great! But how do
you know you're going in the right direction?*

It's a stupid question. The Golden Fort of Jaisalmer
looms in front of our eyes. Where else is there to go?

*Well, at least put something over your face, I call after
her.*

She stops. Pulls an orange sari from the backpack.
Drapes it over her head and across her neck and
shoulders. But instead of letting it hang down, she ties
it under her chest in a big knot. Okay. THAT'S NOT
GOOD. That's going to attract a lot of unnecessary
attention.

Listen, Maya, why don't you fix your sari properly and I'll hold your backpack.

I reach for the strap, but she hits my hand and clasps the bag to her chest. Her eyes narrow into small dark peas.

Fine. I give up. Keep your ratty old bag. I've been trying to help but clearly you don't want any. I get it. Okay?

She doesn't answer. (Why would she?) Instead she looks past my angry face toward the city. As if she knows exactly where she's going.

And I am just a bug under her feet.

Jaisalmer

I was six when I first saw the great saffron fort.
Leaning over the neck of a camel my hands reached
for the enormous golden walls. I cried from the tug
in my chest. As if the city was dragging me home.

Inside the gates the streets hummed like a beehive.
I'd never seen so many people before. I turned to
Barindra and asked, *But where are the goats?*

Everyone in town has heard this story. How a
nomad's son, wearing unbleached cotton, was the
only survivor of a desert storm. How he learned to
read and write, earning the top spot in every one of
his classes. How he appreciated his salvation by being
friendly to all his neighbours.

It's a heartwarming tale. Downright inspiring.
Except for when the hero falls, failing to live up to his
promise. To his myth.

I watch Maya's face as we follow the maze of narrow
streets into the old city. Her eyes soften. And not a
smile, exactly, but something bubbles beneath her
skin. Like an underground stream dampening the
earth.

I've always been curious about water we cannot see.
Running deep and silent, searching the place for

where the earth will yield. Then a surfacing. A birth. Finally freed from the darkness.

I wonder if Maya feels it too? This coming-in-from-the-wilderness.

(Damn this diary! My imagination is turning me into a romantic. The change in Maya's face is from the reflective glow of the yellow stones. That's it.)

Hari

We're almost home when I feel the blow on the back of my head. *Hari.* I spin around, grab his skinny shoulder, and hold him against the wall. *I don't have time for this. I'm already late because of you.*

That's when I notice his eye. Already turning purple from my fist. *Don't worry,* I had assured him after he chased me through the streets, finally catching me in front of Salim Singh's haveli. *Your sister's still a virgin!* The punch was my promise.

Hari looks across my shoulder at Maya. *What's that orange thing standing behind you? Ah, your parents got you a real whore, Sandeep. So now you'll leave my sister alone!*

I push Maya through the door. I'll deal with him later.

Home

There was no time to explain before Amma's hand
slapped my face so hard I cried out for a second time
this morning.

An hour and half to get home from the train station?
What were you doing? Look at her! I told you,
Sandeep, you were not to touch the girl!

My throat goes dry.
I bite down on my anger.
But my mouth feels like it's full
of sunflower husks.
I want to spit into the room.
Blame Maya for the shit I'm in
and the welt swelling
across my cheekbone!
But she lifts her head and looks at me.
The expressionless stare from
the train station is gone.
The stubbornness that
led us home is faded.
Her mask falls.
I see that her real face is a prison of fear.

I am sorry, Amma. Maya was frightened of the
rickshaws. It was necessary for us to walk.
That is why we look so hot and disheveled.

*Frightened of rickshaws? Who ever heard of
such a thing?*

What happened next was a little surprising to
everyone. Maya dropped to her knees and kissed the
hem of Amma's skirt. Then touched her feet.

What will the neighbours say?

According to Dadima, an unmarried girl in a house
with an unmarried man (me) is disgraceful. *A
stranger under our roof. The neighbours will be
clicking their tongues by evening.*

Amma has decided we'll not pass Maya off as a
boy. We refer to her as our cousin from far away.
Where? Where? the neighbours press. *Very far
away!* Amma proclaims loudly. *And that's all you
need to know!* My grandmother was right. The arrival
of the girl with the orange sari twisted into a knot has
not gone unnoticed, and after supper there are
visitors streaming through the kitchen.

She is pregnant, yes, Mina? they ask. *You will
give her rosary pea to take the child away?* No,
no, Amma argues. *Her parents are ill. We are
only taking care of her for a time. Well,* she
doesn't look like a cousin, their probing voices
insinuate. *What happened to her hair? Why
doesn't she speak? What evil takes her voice?*
Cluck. Cluck.

Barindra enters the kitchen to the shock of Amma.
This is rubbish he speaks firmly to the chattering
women. *Accha, accha. Go away. Okay, okay,
Barindra,* they say, and shrug. They bustle to the
door, not waiting until they're outside before

commenting loudly, *What kind of man crosses the threshold of his wife's kitchen? What has happened to the Patel family?*

Tower

Maya is sleeping.
In the small room.
At the top of the house.
Next to burlap sacks.
Rice. Lentils. Corn.
On a rope bed I carried up
three flights of stairs.
(Imagining her body
sinking into the twine.)

Sandeep! You're not to be up here.
Do you understand? Ever.

The welt on my cheek flares.

Amma puts down the tray. Rice. *Dhal.*
A glass of water. She pulls a cover over Maya,
but she kicks it off and tugs her sari
up to her chin. Adoptive mother shrugs.
It doesn't matter to me.

Amma pushes me past the thin cotton curtain and
down the narrow stairwell.
Her fingers dig into my shoulders.

Ow!

Don't forget what I've said.

Yes, Amma.
But sleeping girls weigh
heavy on the brain.

The diary (according to Parvati)

- Are you writing everything down?

- Oh yeah. It's exciting stuff. Maya breathes while she sleeps. Two days of nothing, Deedi!

- Well, she has to wake up eventually. Then you can start with her habits. And ticks.

- Ticks? How strange is this girl?

- Everyone has ticks, Sandeep. For example, you tug your ears when you're upset.

- I don't!

- Repetitive gestures are interesting, that's all. They sometimes reveal trauma or nervousness.

- I think Amma's getting suspicious about the book.

- Tell her you want to be a writer, Sandeep.

AS IF.

But maybe an international spy.

List #1

Maya's habits:
    eating—only water
    nervous behaviour—tugs at hair
    sleeping—all the time; no sheet;
    orange sari

What's that in your hand?

A notebook, Amma.

What's it for?

For writing?

You're not sure?

*I'm sure. I've decided to
become a writer.*

*Aiiii! You are determined to have
no future! Barindra! Have you
heard of Sandeep's latest plan to
waste his life? A WRITER!*

Leave the boy alone, Mina. He'll find his way yet.

What kind of writing, Sandeep?
Amma's face is flushed the colour
of a plum.

Er, poetry?

*Aiii! Even more wasteful! And
stop tugging at your ears! You'll
make them even longer.*

List #2

The contents of Maya's backpack:

sari
slip
secrets
silence
comb

(Is that a poem?)

And no ID at all.

The new prime minister

Barindra hands me the *Hindustan Times*.
Rajiv Gandhi is quoted in bold print: "When a big tree
falls, the earth trembles."

A metaphor? I ask.

Indira Gandhi is the tree, he says. *The rioting in
New Delhi is the earth trembling.*

Earthquake?

*Yes, Sandeep. Our new prime minister compares a
naturally occurring event like seismic activity to
hate crimes and revenge killings. And get this: the
government insists that only 326 people were
killed between November 1 and 7. But I have
heard the total is closer to two thousand!*

So many?

*And Parvati heard five thousand! Yet 326 is the
government's official number. And they claim that
only a few communities were affected. Khichripur,
Punjabi Bagh, and South Delhi. No more. Tell
me, Sandeep, when entire families are wiped out,
how do we forgive ourselves?*

He storms out of the room. It wasn't a question.

I turn back to the paper. Bihar, Madhya Pradesh, Haryana, Uttar Pradesh. There were riots and murders in these states too.

Amma reads the paper over my shoulder. *It's like they couldn't stop.*

Who?

The rioters. They were caught up in a mad frenzy.

You're excusing them?

No. I'm just stating a fact. These things happen in this country. Rightly or wrongly. Mob behaviour is difficult to control.

Not by the army, it isn't! Bahrindra says, returning. *But no one called them! Do you realize that the government did nothing to prevent this slaughter? No politician came forward to denounce the madness!*

But why?

Why? Electoral victory, Sandeep. More votes are won with dissension than peace.

Recurring

I dreamed again of the girl in the
golden sari.

Where are you?

Here.

But I can't see you. It's too dark.

Don't worry. I'm here.

*Say my name. Say my name
and I'll know you're here.*

Maya! Maya!

I woke up.
With Amma staring down at me.

In the night

She's up! The sound of pacing echoes through
the house. Feet thudding like drums. How can a
thin girl be so loud? I look to the sleeping bodies,
but no one else is roused.

A new noise starts, a creaking whine. Like a rope
stretching between an ox and its cart. Dadima rolls
over, but her breathing returns to a low steady
snore.

I run up the stairwell, two steps at a time. A finger
to my lips. *Shhh! Shhh! You'll wake the women,
Maya! Shhh!* A line of spit dribbles down my
chin.

On the top riser I push the curtain back and
see Maya jumping up and down on the cot.
Finally she gets high enough to grab the
edge of the stone wall. Her feet dangle over
the bed. Her head tilts back.

What are you doing? I whisper as loud as I dare.
But I know exactly what she's doing.

She's looking at the night sky from the space
where the wall doesn't meet the roof.

I want to go to her. But to do what? Let her put
her foot on my shoulder? Hold her up so she can

see the slice of white moon swinging over the city
like a cold sun?

(I'm not supposed to be in here and I'm not
supposed to touch her.)

I step past the curtain at the same time she lets go.
She drops down onto the bed. Her legs collapse
under like a foal's.

We look at each other. Tears spill from her eyes
like fallen stars.

Oh dear. She's even beautiful when she cries.

Dressing Maya

She's too skinny, Amma says as Maya slides out
the door to the street. *I had to pleat her sari a
dozen times. It was like dressing a corpse.*

She grabs a pot and starts hitting it with a metal
spoon. *Bang! Bang!* She's erasing the unlucky
words from the air.

*And she's too young to wear that sari! Shall we
have to pay for a salwar and kameez as well as
feed the child?*

The question is for Barindra, who's not here.
He's gone to the post office to mail letters to the
consulates: USA, England, France, Germany,
Italy, Canada, Australia, New Zealand, and Kenya.
The letters ask if a young girl from their country
has been reported missing.

*Go on now, Sandeep. Take her to the market.
Barindra doesn't care what people think, so why
should I? Buy her some sweets. Her bones could
use the fat. And her disposition could use the
honey.*

Yours too, I think, but don't dare say. *All right,
Amma. I could go for some little round ladoos
right about now.*

*Not for you, Sandeep! And don't go to Rashid's
stall!* she shouts after me. *He charges too much!
And tell the girl to keep the scarf on her head!*

I'm surprised we're allowed to go out at all. Maya's of
marriageable age. Her short hair indicates she might
be a widow or a girl of ill repute. But Barindra said,
*Let them go. It'll be fine. We don't live in the Dark
Ages. And besides, we are well respected in this town.*

For some odd reason, Amma doesn't argue. *Oh, I'm
sure the town has moved on to other gossip, Barindra.*

Labyrinth

I let Maya wander. Follow her nose along the
twists and turns of the cobbled streets. A gridless
plan designed to confuse an invading army.

At night, it's almost impossible to navigate this
labyrinth. Familiar landmarks like carved doors,
cantilevered balconies, or a stone elephant's lifted
trunk disappear into shadow when the sun goes
down. But I've done it. More than once. Just last
week after Tejal snuck out of the house to meet me
in the alley. *We'll be together one day,* she
whispered in the darkness, holding my hands
away from her body. *But not now.*

Shit. Hari. I meant to give him a letter for his
sister.

> *Dear Tejal,*
> *Our family is in crisis. My cousin from far*
> *away has come to Jaisalmer for her health.*
> *I cannot see you for a while. Don't doubt*
> *how much you mean to me,*
>> Sandeep

That should do it. Serious. Warm. But uncommitted.

The lists at Manak Chowk Market

Maya finds the way to the market as if she was
flying above the city. Seeing its secret pattern
from the air. I follow a few steps behind, taking
notes.

A list of things Maya stops to look at:
    —black goats tethered to posts
    —red chickens pecking in cages
    —jars filled with crumpled spiders
    —beetles on their backs, hairy legs waving
    —a young Indian man with pen in hand

I turn red. Like a thread of saffron.
    —yellow brass pots, copper bowls
    —turmeric, cinnamon, grey sulfured ginger
    —pearly winged pigeons wanting flight

She glances at my notebook.
    —roasted golden nuts
    —translucent rice
    —raw beef netted with flies

I want to be a writer, I explain lamely,
spinning the fountain pen between
my fingers.
    —coconut oil in thick blue bottles
    —green cotton scarves
    —silver silk, the colour of night sand

You know, Maya, if you want, I could
get you a notebook like this one.

Did that sound casual enough?
Not too pushy?

She shakes her head and walks away.
    —*an angel fallen to earth*

Every eye

Is on Maya.

Hunched-over beggars.
Widows in white.
The blind.
The crippled.
The bird man, hawk on his arm.

They step out of her path.

The seller of old newspapers.
A banker in white and black.
The scribe and his pen, fingers
stained with ink.

But their eyes follow.

Even the homeopath selling sugar for medicine.
And the sweet man pouring honey like water.

Do they see what I see? The perfection of her
face? Or the look of despair that broke Parvati's
heart?

The basket weavers stop weaving.
The tailor puts his needle down.
A monkey handler quiets his beast.
The silversmith lays his hammer on the ground.
Even the sadhu stops his preaching as she passes.

Her silence matches theirs.
But not her innocence.

Goddess

Amma asks how the market went.

(Well, let's see. Shall I tell her that Maya caused a
stir wherever she went? Men blushed and turned
away. The old fell to their knees shaking.
Children held her hand and called her *Lakshmi*.
And one woman actually cursed her, shaking her
bangles like warning bells. And me? I just
followed like a pathetic love-struck servant.)

Went fine, Amma. She kept her scarf on.

(I was almost glad when Hari showed up. Being
with Maya is like floating inside a dream. Time
stops. All I hear is the sound of her breathing.
All I listen for is her voice. *Your face is all mushy,
Sandeep,* Hari said, knocking me on the shoulder
in front of a table piled with green mangoes.
Shall I tell Tejal you've forgotten about her?)

Sandeep! Wake up! I am talking to you!

Oh, what, Amma?

*You're standing in front of me, but you're asleep!
I asked you if Maya bought anything?
I know Parvati gave her some rupees.*

She bought sweets for the children, Amma.

What a wasteful child.

And some flowers for your altar. Marigolds.

Overheard in the sleeping room

*Nothing stirs the girl. She has no
feeling, Barindra. Parvati must be
wrong. She cannot be Sikh. You
know how noisy they are. And
emotional. Angry, shouting and yelling.
Everything except tears.*

*In the last two weeks they've
been hunted like animals,
Mina!*

*I know! And I don't mean
because of their recent troubles.
I mean their natures.*

*They have a strong faith. That
makes them passionate. But I
don't agree that their
temperament is hot.*

*Perhaps. Assassination is a cool
act. But what do you think,
Barindra? Will history thank the
Sikhs who freed India from Indira
Gandhi?*

*And thank them for bringing
us Rajiv Gandhi? With his
mandate to mourn his mother
personally and politically? Do
you remember what happened
during the Emergency? They
say he locked up the Muslims
and cut off their balls.*

Cathy Ostlere 239

Husband! Do not speak to me of such things!

But we must speak of them, Mina. So we don't forget the freedoms she stole.

So you agree that she got what she deserved? Because she didn't hesitate to kill when it suited her?

No. I cannot agree. Murder is never justified. Just as it's not right to look the other way while someone else does it. God granted us life. It's our duty to protect it. For every living being.

And at what cost, Barindra?

At risk to ourselves, when necessary, Mina. If not, our gestures are empty.

Night

Maya is jumping on the cot again. Ropes squealing in
the night like a pained animal.
I run up the stairs and throw back the curtain for the
second night in a row.

Maya, I have an idea.

I drag sacks of rice to the wall, piling them into soft
steps. I bow (embarrassingly deep!), then invite
Maya to climb. At the top she moves over so
there's room for me too.

I know I shouldn't, but I leap up. (If Amma catches
us, I don't know what will happen!)

Together we look out over the clear desert night. A
black-domed sky filled with white glitter. And under
it, glowing in the pale light of the moon, the towering
walls of the Golden Fort.

The parapets, I whisper. *Where the queens walk. I'll
take you there tomorrow.*

Maya sighs. Her breath is warm on my shoulder. But
I shiver. All the way down
my spine.

Shit. I'm a goner.

I begin with stone

*Every block of honey-yellow sandstone was sliced out
of a great quarry and carried on the backs of ten
thousand camels.*

(Big round numbers impress the tourists.)

*For fifty years the trains crossed the desert. The
route littered with the humpless skeletons of beasts
collapsing under the weight.*

(Sacrifice sells.)

*Some say the stone quarry is still out there. An
open grave luring travellers, thieves, and eloping
lovers to its depths.*

(Danger, mystery, illicit sex.)

Maya is unimpressed. She's barely listening to the
speech I've told a hundred times for a five-rupee
fee. (I'm expensive but good.) Instead she stares
at the horizon. The smudged line of soft grey
enters her eyes like a ribbon of smoke.

I talk into the silence between us.

*Like all fortified cities, Jaisalmer has a violent history.
Vats of boiling oil hurled over the invaders' heads.
Mass murder-suicide of women and children upon*

defeat. A poison called halahal. Painful but quick.
A preferable death to enslavement by the victors.

(It's all in the details.)

But my favourite story takes place in the thirteenth
century. Jaisalmer was about to fall to the
emperor of Delhi. The men, dressed in saffron
robes, rode out to meet the army and their certain
death. The women watched from behind the
parapets. Skirts and saris fluttered in the wind.
Hands gripped the yellow sandstone for strength.
Their palms were raw and cut. Blood stained silk
and skin. The women paced while the men were
slaughtered. Husbands. Fathers. Sons.

I kneel down to show Maya where the stone has
worn away. *Touch here and you will see how*
sorrow leaves its mark. Steps of grief wore these
grooves in the ramparts. See? I look up.

Her face is furious.
She bites hard into her lip until
a thread of blood stains the skin.

Stupid stupid stupid

You can make a stone sing, Parvati had said.

I can make a stone cry.

*Oh God, I'm sorry, Maya. That was a terrible
story to tell.*

She turns and walks away from me.

*Maya, please! It was insensitive, I know. I was
trying to show you that I'm a great tour guide
instead of thinking about who was listening.*

Her sari snags on the rough-hewn stones. She
gathers the cloth into her arms like a bedsheet.

*Come on, Maya, slow down! Let me apologize.
Let me make it up to you. Somehow.*

She starts down a long set of stairs to the city below.

Maya!

At the bottom step she pulls the end of the sari
over her head and pushes into a narrow street.

Wait!

She disappears into a crowd. A drip of orange paint.

Lost

I CANNOT BELIEVE IT.

This is my town! And I know every inch! Every
alley, every door, every loose stone in every street
is known to me. There's nowhere to hide that I
haven't already hidden. Under a stall in the
market. In the shadows of the Jain temples.
Behind a carved screen. Under a vegetable cart.
Under a woman's skirt.

I CANNOT BELIEVE I LOST HER.

I ask the children.
The merchants.
The women in the brothel.
I ask the beggars.
The priests.
Even the leper who lost his tongue.
But she is gone.
Into shadow. Into stone.

I knock frantically on the door of every family I
know. Even Tejal's. Hari runs to my house to see
if Maya's returned.

I don't understand.
Who is this girl who can disappear into air?

Three excruciating hours

Before the voices lead me to an alley.

Who are you? You are very pretty.
    A dozen women circling.
But where is your hair?
    Pulling. Tearing.
Given to a god in devotion?
    Pinching. Poking.
Or cut off for your wickedness?
    Spitting in her face.

Stop it! I shout.

Oh ho ho, they chant.
Here is her prince.
    Hooting and laughing.
Come to save the whore!

I push the women aside and
gather Maya into my arms.
Her body trembles like a newborn goat.
Her teeth chatter like a glass wind chime.
Her eyes hold mine, then drown.

I have failed her. She is marked.

Dusk

The last rays of daylight follow us through the open
door of the house. Will the sun be our shield? Protect
us against the certain wrath to come? Maya and I
stand in the hallway. Amma is livid. Eyes black like
a storm.

I can explain, I begin.

I doubt it, she says.

It wasn't our fault.

Is that right, Sandeep?

The unasked question floats.
    THEN WHOSE?

Maya bows to Amma, gathers her sari,
walks slowly up the stairs. Each footstep
acknowledges her guilt.

              FAULT.
        MY.
    WAS.
IT.

Amma

*So what I predicted is finally
here, Sandeep. I knew we
wouldn't get away with Maya.*

> *But it's not her fault the
> women in this town are
> cruel and ignorant!*

*That doesn't change a thing.
There is talk on the street now.
Talk about us. Our family! Who
are we really? Do we have some
secret? Who is this creature
called Maya? So tell me,
Sandeep. Who is she?*

> *I don't know! Why do you
> think I know anything?*

*Because I see you writing in that
book. And you seem to have a lot to say.*

> *My book is my business,
> Amma!*

*Fine, Sandeep. Protect her if
you want, but no more parading
Maya around like she's some
princess. Tomorrow she goes to
work for us. I can pass her off as
a servant easier than a cousin.*

> *What kind of work? Look at
> her hands. This girl isn't a
> labourer!*

*Ah, you-of-no-caste all of a
sudden feel that such work is
demeaning. All that education
from Barindra about Gandhi's
classless society and here you
are, ready to judge! She will
help with the laundry. And if it's
too far beneath her caste, I'm
sure she'll let us know.*

*But you cannot be serious!
The other women will torment
her! Pita will not allow it, Amma.*

*Of course your father will. He loves
to put his philosophies into
practice. And Maya is his latest
project on compassion and
acceptance.*

*And she is your project
for meanness!*

*I know you think I'm out to get
Maya. But you're wrong. The
girl doesn't know how to help
herself. So I will force her to
speak out of her agony.*

November 22–29, 1984

Why is there so much misery in the world? — M.

She writes

My greatest fear—
    What if someone reads this diary?

Has become my greatest hope—
    She writes. To me.

When?
Last night?
While I slept?
Did she come downstairs?
Slip the book from under my head?
Or did I leave it out?
By accident?
On purpose?

OH SHIT.
The other greatest fear—
    She knows I'm an idiot?

Did she read all my words?
Every page? Every thought?

And now what?
A response?
And what a question!
    Why is there so much misery in the world?

I must answer her.
Press the pen's nib to the page.

(Just as she did.)
But what?
What's the answer?
The words to soothe her.

(Pain, Maya. It's the only reason I can think of. I'm sorry. —S.)

Laundry

When I was a little boy, I liked to watch the
women wash laundry at the Gadsisar Sagar Tank.
Beating the scarves and skirts and saris against the
stones, laying them to dry in coloured rows.
Sometimes flocks of birds swooped over. White
feathers falling onto the striped shoreline.

My favourite part was when the women
joined in pairs. Swinging the bands of cloth,
walking toward each other, folding saris and
turbans in half. Then half again. And again.
Until they touched. A square of bright
colour floating in their palms.

Sometimes the wind sang through the
cotton.

I like it when the wind blows. —M.
(I don't. —S.)

What is written

This isn't just my diary anymore.

My secrets, if I had any, are out.
The embarrassing stuff too.
And yet I don't mind.

She writes!

Maybe she's forgiven me.
For frightening her. For losing her.

(She smiled from the kitchen
when Amma had her back turned.)

This is now a shared book.
I like the idea.
But how do you write honestly
if you know someone is going to read it?

Be your self. Please. —M.
(I'm not sure I've ever known who that is. —S.)

Hari

I follow Amma and Maya through the streets in the early morning. Maya carries a bundle of clothes on her head. Holding it with two hands.

Go home, Sandeep, Amma says. *What kind of man watches women do laundry?*

I retreat in a sulk but decide not to go far. I sit at the top of the tank's stone steps and keep my eye on Maya. But my attention is distracted when Hari plants himself beside me.

My stupid sister is still infatuated with you.

No, she isn't.

Well, here, read her letter for yourself.

I shake my head. *Take the letter back and tell her she's too good for me. I don't deserve her.*

Well, it's true, you don't. But she'll be angry if I return it unopened.

Then open it yourself and tell her I read it. I'm busy, Hari. I'm busy with other things.

Ah, the girl, he says, laughing. *Everyone's talking about her. Even Tejal. So when are you going to tell me the truth? That your sister found her in a brothel?*

My hands grip Hari's neck so quickly I'm not sure who's more surprised. I squeeze slowly. Is it easy to kill someone?

When I let go, Hari rolls on the ground, holding his throat. *What's happened to you?* he whispers between coughs. *You've changed since that girl came!*

Hari, I'm sorry. Really really sorry. And it's true. I'm not myself these days. But I can't let you say those things about Maya!

But everyone is saying them, Sandeep! Are you planning to fight the whole town? Wake up! There's talk going around that this girl has put a spell on your family. And you know what that means.

He runs down the steps and is gone. I turn back to Maya. She is spreading a skirt on the ground to dry. Opening the folds into a giant red poppy. When she's done, a woman drags her feet over the flower.

I am the cause of so much trouble. —M.
(No. We are a backward nation. —S.

Second day

Amma forbids me to come down to the tank again. *It's not right, Sandeep. The women are saying the most disgusting things.*

But I follow anyway. I'd rather deal with Amma's anger than leave Maya alone with the gossips. Though some protector I am. I sit and listen. And do nothing.

Paagal! The end of a sari hits Maya across the back of her legs. *You are a crazy one!*

Maya keeps her head down. She beats a red cloth against the rocks.

Suchait hona! A woman kicks dirt across a freshly washed blouse. *We must beware of you!*

I run down the steps, but Amma holds me back. *No, Sandeep!*

I hear the women laugh as Maya struggles with the mound of wet cotton. Twisting and twisting until it weeps with water the colour of blood.

Their cruelty is so easy. —M.
(They've never met anyone like you. —S.)

KARMA

Argument

Maya can barely stand. Cannot eat. She lies on the
bed staring at the space between roof and wall. And
doesn't blink.

Barindra and I argue with Amma.

The child is exhausted, Mina.

And the women are nasty!

*It'll get easier for her, Amma says. Once she
learns how to wring the water out.*

*But she's even thinner, Mina. Shrinking. As if her skin
is giving up whatever fight she's in.*

*And haven't you noticed, Amma? How she lifts
laundry like she's carrying the dead?*

*Your writing is addling your head, Sandeep. You
imagine things that aren't there. And you,
Barindra, what do you know about women's work?
What Maya needs to do is to stop fighting her fate.
Forget her pain. Like the rest of us.*

_____

Yes. Forget. Forgotten. **—M.**
(Forget what? — S.)

Saturday phone call

Parvati says I must hurry.

> - *I know it's only been ten days, but if Maya doesn't tell
> you something soon, she'll spend the rest of her life
> doing laundry! Have you learned nothing, Sandeep?*

My voice is despondent.

> - *Sometimes she flicks her fingers. Like she's playing
> an instrument. Maybe a piano.*

Parvati pauses.

> - *A piano doesn't exactly narrow down the
> country of origin. Anything else?*

I can't tell her what's happening in the pages of the
diary. Yet I hate lying.

> - *Don't give up, brother. I have faith in you.
> How are you sleeping?*

She always asks this. My doctor-sister believes
my dreams come from memories trying to push
their way through to consciousness.

> - *Your body wants to remember,* she says
> softly.

I had to quit school because I lost the ability to focus.

    - I'm sleeping all right, Deedi. Another lie.

Memory

What should a six-year-old remember? The lap of his mother? Her face? But perhaps she was covered. Because of the dust.

/

Parvati said everyone died. Seven people. The bodies found hundreds of feet from the camp. Every one of them alone. Except me. The goats had herded themselves. I must have crawled under their bellies.

It's an unusual story. Nomadic tribes know how to protect themselves from desert storms. But these shepherds seemed to be caught by surprise. Out in the open.

What do you think happened? I asked her.

Maybe one day you'll remember, Sandeep

I hear you at night. —M.
(I don't know why I call out your name. —S.)

Tongues

*Men don't understand that women
are not separate. We're the
community. We're the shared work.
And yes, we are the gossip. But
without each other we die! Men live
only for themselves. Their hearts
beat alone.*

Amma continues to argue hard
with her hand on my wrist.

*Even you, Sandeep, who don't listen
to anyone. You live as if it doesn't
matter that we have a strange girl in
our house. You live as if the gossips
won't come after you next!*

*Stop it, Mina! Leave the boy
alone! These are the tongues
of wicked women. The talk that
you haven't discouraged!*

*It's the women at the laundry.
I say nothing, Barindra.*

*Well, the laundry is finished.
Maya's not our servant, and you
can't just keep her here to wash
blouses, skirts, and dhotis.*

*Fine. But you must admit there's
something unearthly about her,
husband.*

Barindra's face darkens like ink flooding his veins.

Her extraordinary beauty?

That's not all of it. The women are saying that when she walks she makes no footprints.

Ridiculous superstition. We won't fall for that.

Easy for you. People are saying she'll bring misfortune to this town.

So stop listening, Mina. Has no one considered that Maya may have nowhere to go?

And have you not considered that her family threw her out for good reason?

No. I believe she is lost. And it's not safe for her to return home.

All I know, Barindra, is that when I look at that girl I don't see her missing anyone. It's as if she was born into this world alone.

Well, you're right about something, Mina. She's the loneliest creature I've ever seen.

And you wait and see. Something terrible is going to happen.

*Trouble follows that girl like a
shadow.*

What does the fate of one girl even matter? —M.
(You matter. To me. —S.)

A different kind of goat

Amma says we are losing our social standing with each passing day.

Dadima says the mobs will drag the girl away, strip her naked, make her eat shit, then stone her.

Barindra says we are losing our good sense and our moral strength.

My sister says Maya is being singled out as if she carries some communal sin on her skin. Parvati uses the English word: *scapegoat.* Someone who carries the blame for the guilty.

   - What happens to the goat, Deedi?

   - It gets sent to the wilderness. Alone.

Maya won't get out of bed.

The sleeping girl

Amma can't rouse Maya.
Even with her red lamb curry.

Barindra brings a doctor to listen to her heart.
Yes, it's broken, he says. *There's nothing to be
done about that.*

Dadima sneaks an old wrinkled shaman into the
house. *Is the girl a witch?*

I cannot say yes or no, he says. *I can only tell
people what to look for.* (Coward.) He lifts
Maya's hands, turns the palms upward. *Too many
lines,* he says, shaking his head. *She carries an
extra soul. A soul she can't put down.* He drops
angelica oil onto her third eye.

Dadima whispers: *If she dies in our home, will there
be two ghosts to haunt us?*

_____

(Maya? Are you there? –S.)

Rumour #1

In the night all the apples on the trees in Bara Bagh
fell to the ground. The earth shuddered under the
pounding. Someone says they saw a witch dressed in
orange spitting on the fruit.

Fact

A violent wind can harvest an orchard,
Barindra says. *Shake every fruit loose.*
There's nothing supernatural about it.

Rumour #2

A bride in Jaisalmer fainted the night of her marriage
and cannot be wakened. In her sleep, she cries:
Maya. Maya. Where is my husband?

Fact

Just another nervous bride, Barindra
says. *Afraid of the wedding night.
Nothing more to that story.*

Rumour #3

A sand snake was found curled under the body of a
sleeping child. When the little boy woke, the viper bit
his arms, legs, and face. He cried out only once.
Then the snake put his head inside his mouth.

Fact

*Twenty children a year die of
snake bites, Barindra says.
It's not sorcery. It's a door left open.*

Rumour #4

A man claims she came to him in the night.
A naked succubus wanting his body and soul.
And now she has taken all his strength.

Fact

*The man is well known at the
brothel, Barindra says. And yet he
blames Maya for his impotence!*

Rumour #5

A woman who bumped into Maya at the market
died on Tuesday. Two days later she rose from
her funeral pyre and walked into the desert.
Her skin burned green.

Fact

Well, that's just stupid,
says Barindra.

Rumour #6

The word *tonahi* is on everyone's lips. Witch.

Fact

A woman spits on Amma's
head at the market.

The spice man shouts
at her and waves a stem
of wormwood in her face.

Rocks are pitting our front door.

In fear

We are done with this!

Mina, be reasonable. Children die in Jaisalmer every week. Brides refuse to sleep with their husbands. Winds shake trees. Hallucinations can plague the mourning. And men lie about their desire.

And people in fear do terrible things, Barindra. The town believes Maya is not who she appears to be. They claim she casts no shadow. They say that her teeth grow longer as the sun sets.

Yes. Yes. Let me guess what else. She is sleeping with their husbands. This has to stop.

How? How will this stop? Every year there's a story about a witch living in our midst.

And that is what they are— stories! Someone wants to get back at a woman. She spurned a man's advances. She holds title to a property that someone covets. Or the woman is a Dalit with no caste at all. These are the witches, Mina. They are

*powerless victims, nothing
more.*

*And when they come for her, what
will you do? When they throw the
stones? When they beat her? How
will you stop that? You and
Sandeep cannot hold back a mob.
And that is what is coming to our
door. Tonight. Tomorrow. In the
middle of the night.*

Mina . . . .

*Take her. Take Maya away now.
Before our life here is lost.*

Wake up, Maya

Please.
You can't sleep any more.
You've got to wake up.
And tell me what to do.

November 30, 1984

Overheard at the Jaisalmer gate

I smell the camels before I see them.
Mounds of shadow kneeling in the darkness.

Where is Farooq? I hear Barindra whisper to a
tall figure standing beside the beasts.

The young man bows. *I am Akbar. Tenth grandson*
of Farooq. I am sorry to carry news of his sudden illness.

Illness? I spoke to my old friend less than five hours
ago! He seemed well enough.

A very bad case of loose motion. There is no riding
of the camels in such a condition.

So he sent you?

I am to assure you that I am as excellent a guide as
my grandfather. You are not to worry. He bows again.

Well, we shall see. Whether I worry or not. Have
we met before?

Never. I grew up in the desert. I have come to Jaisalmer
for one year only. To study. To improve myself.

He's lying. I don't know how I know. But I can hear
it. The lie rattling in his throat like an apricot pit.

Grandfather has explained the problem, Mr.
Barindra. And he thought I was well suited to the
task. Farooq is an aged man. Not as quick as I.

Akbar takes a step toward Barindra. *You are in*
good hands.

Barindra steps back.
Now I can see Maya.
Wrapped in grey.
Her face shadowed by folds of wool.
One shaking hand keeps the blanket from
falling.

Ah, so this is the girl everyone is talking about?
Akbar bows. His turban almost touches the
ground. *Yes, she is beautiful. See, even the moon*
adores her. As if on command, a single cloud
clears and a soft light washes over Maya's face.
But is she Indian? Hmm. I think not. From another
place. A country with a big sky. And no monsoons,
perhaps.

His voice is smooth as silk.
No one is breathing.
Is Barindra going to fall for this bullshit?

That's enough, Akbar, I say, with a tone I might
use with servants. (If I had any.) I step out of
my hiding place behind the fort wall

Brother

Sandeep! says Barindra. *What are you doing here? I told you not to follow me. You were to stay home where you're needed!*

But I've taken care of that, Pita. Hari is there. If a mob comes he will show them the empty attic. He will even send for the police so Amma and Dadima will be safe.

(The deal with Hari came at a price. A promise to leave Tejal alone. I felt a little bad for the extravagance of my false tears. His sister is beautiful but silly. And doesn't hold a candle to Maya.)

So you have left your duty to someone else? This is how you repay your adoptive mother after all she has done for you? Not good enough, Sandeep! What kind of son are you?

With all respect, Pita, I am indebted to my sister too. I promised Parvati I would watch over Maya. To never to leave her alone.

Ah, a dutiful brother, says Akbar. *Something the family can be proud of.*

Protector

Who do you think you are speaking to? I say to
Akbar. *For a camel driver, you are far too familiar!*

*Oh, I do apologize. But I feel like we have met.
You see, I know who you are. The famous tour
guide, Sandeep of Jaisalmer. The boy who was
saved by goats. And though you are a cheeky son
you appear to be a thoughtful sibling.* He laughs.
*And perhaps a protector of young women too? A
Vishnu to Maya's Lakshmi?*

I'm glad it's dark so Maya can't see my face
burn.

*I think you are a complicated boy, Sandeep. With
an interesting story.*

His deep voice cements me to the earth. A
sinking feeling in my stomach.

I turn to my father. *Pita,* I manage to whisper. *I
will walk or ride the camel that carries the supplies.
I am determined to accompany you.*

Akbar laughs some more. *There's no saddle,
Sandeep. You won't last a mile.*

*I will last, Akbar. I was born in the desert. As you
you've no doubt heard.*

Ah. Well, Barindra Sahib, this adopted son of yours amuses me. We can take him if you're willing. I have another camel.

Barindra looks pained with the decision.

Both of you have left me little choice. The sun is almost up and our departure will be noticed if we don't leave soon. I have no time to check out Akbar's story. Or drag my son back to his house. So we will go. Just don't make me sorry.

Akbar bows to Barindra.
(What a fake.)

I bow to Maya.
(I won't leave you alone with this creep!)

She tugs the blanket over her forehead. But her hand is still.

Go on, Sandeep. Akbar points at a small furclotted camel. *Moomal is waiting for you.*
I'm sure she's happy you're here.

Jerk.

To the desert

Akbar guides Maya toward the largest of the
camels. Brightly coloured tassels and small
silver bells hang from the bridle. The animal
looks ridiculous. Overly adorned. But I can't
help being envious. Mohindra — even the
name is grand — looks princely. Moomal
resembles an insect-eaten rodent with stick
legs.

*So, Maya, are you ready? Akbar asks. For real
silence?* He puts a hand on her back but she
bats it away. *As you wish, princess.* She swings
a leg over the leather seat. Akbar slides in
behind and puts his mouth near her ear. *Don't
worry,* his tongue slithers. *You don't have to
speak in the desert. The sand and wind swallow all
words and deeds.*

Maya shivers.

(Why isn't Barindra saying anything!)

And you, Sandeep. Are you also ready? Three sets
of eyes watch as I struggle with Moomal. *Do
you need to know the magic camel word for UP?*

*Of course not, Akbar! I've been riding since I was a
child.*

He laughs and puts the whip on Mohindra.
Then try to keep up, little man.

I click my tongue, slam my knees, and wave my
tattered whip until Moomal finally drags herself
to standing with a loud angry groan. Akbar and
Maya are already fading into the darkness.

Farooq would have let Maya ride with me!

The great unknown

We travel with the dawn on our shoulder. The thin line
of sunrise crests the horizon. Like a slice of red melon.
Falling from a knife's blade.

Melon! My stomach growls for the sweet
ripe fruit.

Will we stop soon for nashta?

*That depends, Sandeep. Did you bring food? We
weren't planning to feed a fourth.*

(Is this how it will be? Always made to look the fool?)

*No, you misunderstood me, Akbar. At Mool Sagar there
is a tree. Heavy with mangoes. We can fill our bellies
and a sack for later. It is not so much farther from here.*

I remember this tree, says Barindra. *A good idea,
Sandeep.*

You see? I will not be a burden.

I look to Maya. Shrouded like a prisoner. She is
leaning forward. As if trying to get as far from
Akbar as she can.

Mool Sagar

I take out my knife and slice the mangoes
expertly, like Amma taught.
Two cuts to release the seed.
Flesh scored into cubes.
We eat in silence under the tree.

Maya-bati, says Barindra.

I look up. Juice dribbles from my open mouth.
Barindra will address Maya directly?

*Do you understand that we had to take you out of
the city for your own good?*

She keeps her eyes down.

*This can't go on, Maya, says Barindra. Your
silence is dangerous for you.*

We have all stopped eating.
We are quiet.
Waiting for her answer.

Suddenly, a violent squawking rattles the tree
and loosens a flurry of leaves onto our heads.
Akbar picks up a stone and flings it into the
glossy foliage.

Perhaps it is the unknown she is afraid of? Akbar

shouts into the tree.

Maya flinches at the sound of impact.

*Or is there something else at the root of every one
of us?* He throws a second stone. *A question
that haunts our dreams.*

A white parrot flies frantically out of the tree.

How do we name our guilt? Akbar whispers.

Maya's mouth quivers like someone's tugging
on her lower lip. I look away. She might as well
be naked.

(Help.)

I stand up. Stretch my arms out wide to the
empty horizon. *Do not be afraid of limitless
possibilities. The desert is infinite to the eye as
love is to the heart.*

Who taught you that? Barindra asks.

You did.

Barindra shakes his head.

Well, it's a wise statement, says Akbar. *Perhaps
someone from your mysterious childhood?*

I decide to ignore him. I look over my shoulder at Maya. Her fingers are clenched. Red from twisting a scarf in her hands. Was it enough? Did I buy her secret a little more time?

A race

The horizon stretches as we travel west. An
elastic band cutting sky and earth in two. The
camels mark the terrain with their soft pads.
Like rows of stitches mending tears in the land.

The morning drags on. Into afternoon. Sun
climbing, a yellow balloon. The camels lope, the
heat beats down, my head nods and bounces off
my chest. Spit drools from my mouth like a
toothless woman dozing on a bus. Hard to
believe I'm the son of a nomad.

I look over at Akbar riding with one hand on the
reins and another on Maya's hip. She is leaning
against him, her head tucked under his chin,
asleep. Has she so easily fallen under his spell?

Akbar looks over at me, grinning.

When the sand hills break through the horizon
line with their soft ochre peaks, Akbar calls out,
We'll camp tonight in their shadow.

I glance my whip across Moomal's shoulder.
*Shall we race then, Akbar? Last one to the dunes,
unpacks the camels?*

But you are only one small boy! he calls out. *And
we are burdened with two!*

I urge Moomal to go faster.

But you are old and skinny, Akbar, already dry like an old tree!

Yes, that is true, little brother with dung beetle breath! And you know what else is true?

What, my wrinkled friend who rides the farting camel?

Moomal is lazy! Like you!

Akbar hits Mohindra only once and the camel gallops past me like an awkward racehorse.

Maya's scarf falls from her head. Her smile cuts me to the quick. Is she lost to me?

Nothing

This has nothing to do with you, Sandeep.

I've never seen Barindra like this. So decisive. So unwavering. So unsympathetic.

I suppose Akbar knows our destination.

Of course.

But you won't tell me.

No.

And you don't think it's strange that Farooq took ill so quickly? And even stranger that you've never met Farooq's tenth grandson?

I'll watch him, Sandeep. I promise. Now could you please honour your bet and unpack the camels.

The problem with Barindra is that he always thinks the best of people.

After I drive the pegs for Maya's tent into the soft earth, I look for an opportunity to slip her the notebook. What's she thinking? About our guide's wandering hands. And the fact that we don't know where he's leading us.

But Akbar is watching me. Like a hawk and I'm
the rodent for his lunch.

And I don't dare take the chance.

The dune

Sand like silk under our feet.

Maya and I make our way up the dune slowly.
Heads down, feet sliding back with each step. I
watch her make small adjustments with her body.
Straightening her back, bending her elbows,
lifting her knees. Soon she is scrambling like a
sand crab. And I am right behind her.

When we get to the top I put a leg on each
side of the ridge. *Do you see it, Maya? It's
the sea!* I point to the horizon, to the air
weaving and moving in the heat. It's an old
game I used to play when Barindra took us
on desert treks. *I'm going to cross that water
one day, Deedi. I know you will,* my sister
agreed.

Maya, there's something I want to say to you, I
begin. *About Akbar.*

But the dune wakes like a shape-shifting
beast straightening its back. And the peak
crumbles under our feet.

My eyes sting as I'm thrown down the
flanks. Hands reaching for something solid
to grab. Mouth filling with sand. Oh, if only

my ears would fill too, and I wouldn't have
to listen to Akbar's taunting!

*Sandeep! I don't think that's the way to watch
over your Lakshmi! Headfirst!*

I come to a stop at Akbar's feet.

Good thing I'm here, he says. *You keep falling
down on your job.*

He helps Maya to her feet. She's covered
with sand. And her sari has become
undone.

Kind of fun, isn't it, Maya? He speaks to her
but looks at me.

But she's not smiling. She's clutching folds
of orange in her hand.

Sunset

The day burns itself out behind the dunes. The
last rays of sun piece the ridge like a bloodred
crown.

Maya is sitting on the ground beside her tent.
Her palms are turned upward. She lifts them
like she's offering something to the sky.

I lean over and place my hands under hers.
The sand runs through our fingers. A soft
stream. Into the folds of her sari.

The poem is on my lips without thinking:
    "O man, know this to be truth—
    The world is a dream,
    Any moment it may pass away;
    Thou has built a house of sand,
    How can it endure?"

Nanak? Akbar asks.

Yes.

Continue. You have a nice voice.

No, that's enough.

Okay. I think I know the rest anyway:
    "How can it endure?

All this is Maya.
O simpleton, why art thou entangled in
delusion?
Wake up! Wake up, lest it be too late."

Akbar and I stare.
Eyes locked like two animals
sizing each other up.
Whoever moves first will lose.

Sand

The wind blows through the camp and chases the
shadows away. The desert is quiet again except for
the sound of sand sweeping across the dunes.

I know I shouldn't but I rub my eye. Grinding the
grit into my cornea.

Maya puts her hand on my shoulder. Then a fingertip
on my eyelid. She holds it closed.

I feel her breath on my cheek. We wait for the
tears to fill and carry the grain away.

I wake up.

Morning

So, Sandeep, you are finally up, Akbar calls. *Did you have a
pleasant dream? We heard you wailing all night
long.*

Shut up, Akbar.

*Maya is on her knees. Holding a long green cloth
in her hands. Akbar is showing her how to twist
the cotton and wrap it into a nomad's turban. A
thick coiled snake is taking shape on Akbar's big
fat head.*

Maya, he whispers. *Maya.*

I feel my shoulder tighten like a slingshot. My
fist rises. Ready to fire into his jaw, splitting
bone and flesh, but then I see Maya's face.
Something has changed since yesterday. Her
eyes are flat. Like a light dimming

I try to think of a sharp comeback instead of breaking
Akbar's nose, but I can't form the words.
My brain has been cut off from my body.

When I lower my arm, all I can imagine is the end of
that stupid turban stuffed down his throat.

December 1–2, 1984

The Thar Desert

We travel. We rest. We travel again. Akbar sings.
Such is the rhythm of the desert dweller. Such is his
pleasure and restlessness.

Rumi? asks Barindra.

No. Those are the words of the great poet, Akbar. He
is talented, yes?

(He is an asshole, no?)

Sandeep! Akbar calls to me. *You will share another*
poem with us while we ride?

I refuse. To even open my mouth around that man
invites ridicule. But in my mind, I silently repeat the
words of the Persian poet al-Hallaj:

> *For your sake, I hurry over land and water*

> *For your sake, I cross the desert and split the mountain in two*

> *And turn my face from all things*

> *Until the time I reach the place*

> *Where I am alone with you.*

I glance over at Maya. She's staring across the desert.
Not at me.

What did you think, Sandeep? I scold myself, silently.
That she could read your mind?

I sound like Akbar. Inside my head.

Desert tales

Tell us your story, Akbar, Barindra says. To pass the time. We know nothing about you.

Yes, Akbar, I call. Who do you say you are? And why haven't I seen you in Jaisalmer?

Because you and I are different, Sandeep. I stick to myself. You live in a pack. I study music and literature when the shadows are long. You bask in the sun like a stray dog. You bargain with the market sellers. Entice tourists to pay for your overpriced guiding. And seduce girls when you're not trying to separate a rupee from some poor soul. Unlike you, Sandeep, I've tried to do the best with the small gifts God gave me.

Ah, yes, you're a poet. A poor but spiritually elevated life. You sing about the world but don't live in it.

We can't all have your advantages, Sandeep. To be rescued so miraculously. Given a new and better life.

And you choose to live through other's stories, Akbar.

I collect them, Sandeep. Yours is a particularly

*good one. Nomads rarely die in sandstorms. That
is interesting*

*Maybe the story is better if they're fishermen from
the Arabian Sea. Trying a career change.*

*You make fun as if they don't matter to you at all,
Sandeep! Do you not remember anything of what
happened?*

*Is that why you came to Jaisalmer? To pluck my
memories for a song? It's odd to be so interested in
other people's histories, Akbar. Have you nothing
else in your life but old desert tales?*

*No, Sandeep. Unlike you. But that will change.
Sooner than you think*

Fresh tracks

We'll stop here for two nights, Akbar says when we
arrive at a range of sand dunes blocking the sky.
I'm getting sore.

Yes, it must be uncomfortable, I think bitterly.
His hand sliding over Maya's thigh. Pulling her
against him when she nods off. Pressing her
waist when Mohindra trips. He sings in her ear
all day long. And Barindra doesn't say a thing!
Like *he's* the servant now!

Even Maya no longer flinches at Akbar's touch.
Has she given in? Given up?

Maya looks at no one now. Stares ahead at the
horizon of this dead landscape. Her body still.
Fingers silent as if the music under her skin has
been forgotten.

She is fading. Fading. Into dust. How long until
I reach for her and find her gone? Slipped off
Mohindra's back. The thin wrapped body lying
on the ground. Buzzards circling.

The desert could bury her in a day. Flesh
returned to earth.

What does the fate of one girl even matter? she
wrote in this book.

(I am concocting a plan to tie Mohindra and
Akbar together with his turban! And then run!)

Each man

I wish you'd stop him, Pita.

Stop?

Akbar.

From cooking our meal? Tending to the camels?

From guiding us to nowhere! I doubt even you know where we're going now! And he taunts. Makes me look like a fool.

You'll find a way, Sandeep.

A way to what?

To match him. Make yourself his equal. Each man has different strengths.

I don't see strengths. I see cunning. Akbar is no regular guide, Barindra. And I don't believe he is simply helping out Farooq. He's after something.

Perhaps, Sandeep. But who in this world doesn't have some motivation?

Pita, why are you so blind? He's after Maya!

Is that so? And what about you, Sandeep? What are

you after? What are you doing out here in the desert
if it isn't about Maya? What are any of us doing
here?

He kicks at the sand. And walks away.

What indeed?

It's not like Tejal.
(I really did want her flesh under my hands.)
And it's not just Maya's beauty.
(Though I can't deny my desire.)
I'm not here because of a promise to my sister.
(That fooled no one.)

So what am I doing? In the middle of the desert
with a stranger who hates me, a father who's
losing his morality, and a girl who is almost a
mirage?

Barindra taught me that we are not to get in the
way of a soul's path. Respect. Witness. Bow
down to its greater knowledge. And never impose
our will.

But what if the body that houses the soul is selfdestructive?
Do we stand by and do nothing?

Actually it's quite simple, Sandeep, Parvati assured
me. *This is how you will help her. Be Maya's voice.
Until her own returns.*

But what if that never happens?
I cried out so I could be discovered.
If Maya, makes no sound, how can she be saved?

December 3, 1984

The loneliest

Akbar and Barindra are packing up the camels.
Another day under a blistering sun. Another
day closer to the unknown destination. And
another day of Akbar's voice singing the
melancholic songs of the desert. I wish he
wasn't so good. Each perfect note soothes my
anger. He seduces even me to follow him
blindly across the sand.

I find Maya sitting by herself next to Moomal.
The ragged camel is chewing on leaves, his
large mouth mashing in wet circles.

Maya? I try to invoke a commanding (*I'm the
only one who can help you now!*) but soft (*I would
never hurt you*) tone.

*Maya, I would like you to write in my notebook.
Your name. Where you're from. And where you
would like to go. I am sure that once Barindra has
this information we will be able to turn around, get
out this desert, and find you a place where you will
be safe.*

She lifts her head but looks past me or is it
through me.

(*So, Sandeep. Now you're bossy, too?*)

She turns her gaze back to the circles and spirals she's drawing in the sand. Lines that don't close.

I am chastened. By her voice in my head.

All right then, Maya. No words. We're in the desert. Who needs words?

I break a branch from the tree, tear off the leaves for Moomal, then mark New Delhi, Karachi, Jodhpur, and Jaisalmer in the sand. I draw a border at the edge of the Thar Desert. Then I widen the map to include Bombay, London, Singapore, New York.

Show me, I whisper. Please. *While Barindra and Akbar are busy.*

Without looking at me she stands up, takes the stick, and holds it over the crude map. I hear her inhale. Watch her tighten her grip. But her hands start to quiver.

Just point, Maya. Where are you from?

She takes a step to the left. London? But the stick starts swinging violently. Back and forth between Delhi and New York. Even a shaman's divining rod doesn't vibrate this hard!

Were the gossips right? Is Maya possessed?

I place my hands on her wrists and the
trembling stops. No. She has no supernatural
power. And there's no underground river below
our feet. It's fear alive in every muscle in her
body. Holding her captive.

She pushes my hands away. Breaks the stick
across her knees and throws it to the ground.

It's all right, Maya. It'll be okay. I promise.

She flings open the tent flap and disappears
inside.

(Really? How is this ever going to be okay?)

Knife

What's the matter, Sandeep? Has your Lakshmi refused her love?

Go away, Akbar.

She's really something, isn't she? The way she gets under the skin. Especially here. He taps a purple bruise on his cheek.

What are you talking about?

She hit me. A simple misunderstanding. But you've been so wrapped up in your deep feelings, you didn't even notice.

I noticed! I thought one of your smelly camels kicked you!

Listen, Sandeep, and learn. You and your father have brought her out to the desert. And for what? You think all this emptiness will make her speak to you? Pour out her heart? What she wants is to be rescued. By a man.

What did you do to her, Akbar?

Nothing you wouldn't do if you had the guts.

The knife is in my hand without me reaching for it.

Oh, Sandeep, you are truly pitiable.

If I slit your stomach open, Akbar, all I'd find is a snake pit!

Put the knife away, boy. And I'll give you some more advice. Forget about her. Her fate is sealed. Surely you've figured that out by now.

Not if I can help it!

What can you do, Sandeep? You're a boy and you're in over your head. What's so particularly pathetic is your innocence. There's only one outcome for this situation. At least Barindra figured that out days ago.

Truth

I have no choice, Sandeep, Barindra whispers.
This is not what I wanted to do. But I can't find
another way out of this mess. I can't take Maya
back to Jaisalmer. Your mother won't have her and
neither will anyone else.

But who gave you the right? To give away this
daughter who is not your daughter? And to Akbar?

I'm not giving her to Akbar. She will live with his
family until she decides her own fate.

She will become their servant! Their slave! She
will never be able to get away from them even if
she wants to! You know this!

Sandeep, I gave her safety and asylum for as long
as I could! When Farooq offered to take her to his
village it seemed like the best choice under the
circumstances. If Maya wants to change her
destiny then she'd better speak up fast. We will
arrive in Alamar tonight. And then we are done.

Please, Pita. Just give me a little more time.
Another day. Look. Look at my book. See? Maya's
written to me. Before. She was starting to trust me
and then you yanked her out here to the desert!

Let me see that book, Sandeep.

Keep your hands off, Akbar!

*Barindra, make him give it to me. Maybe there's
something in it that will actually help Maya.*

*No, Akbar! So far, I have let you guide us across
the desert in spite of your questionable story about
Farooq taking ill. I've looked away when you've
been too familiar with Maya. And I've done nothing
to stop you from tormenting Sandeep. Because I
needed you. But I draw the line here. You may not
have my son's diary! A man's writing is his soul!*

*Barindra's eyes are red. Blood vessels
bursting. He stares until Akbar lowers his gaze.*

Fine.

*Good. Then there's nothing else to say. Let's pack
these camels and get on our way.*

*Akbar waits until Barindra is on the other side
of the camp. A reminder to you, Sandeep? Stay
away from my future wife.*

Easy

I lunge. Akbar takes the blade across his wrist.

Shit, Sandeep! What are you doing?

We both stop and stare at the bright river of blood
flowing to the sand. A ribbon joining man to earth.

I fall to my knees. The knife drops. I was wrong.
It's not easy to kill someone.

I hear Maya's breath beside me. Quick. Panicked.
Her lips are swollen. Almost bruised. Like
she's been biting down hard. *I'm sorry, Sandeep.*
Her voice in my head.

(I'm sorry. I'm sorry. I'm sorry.)

She takes my hand. But I can't hold back the tears
any longer.

Hey, I'm the one who's bleeding here! Akbar shouts.

Well, you deserved it, says Barindra. *Why can't you
leave the boy alone?* He presses on Akbar's wound.
Blood seeps between his fingers.

You know what's kind of sad, Sandeep? says Akbar.
*You were Maya's best hope. The charismatic boy who
might have convinced her to say who she is. But you*

failed. Instead you made Maya think she was safe in her silence. She trusted you and all you've done is deliver her into the wilds of the desert. And me.

Is it true? I lift my head to look at Maya. Did I betray her with my own desire?

I watch tears fall from the tips of her dark lashes. Silver beads of sorrow.

(The world is a dream.)

Wake up, Sandeep, says Akbar. Your girlfriend is out of options. She's going with me.

Dogs

We fight like rabid dogs. No teeth but fists
hammering in successive beats. A steady
cadence of rage and sorrow. Akbar's wound is
open and weeping. I can taste his blood in my
mouth.

Stop it! Barindra shouts at us. *Stop it! Stop it!*
Can you not see what is happening? Maya's gone!

His voice pierces through the fog of torn flesh
and blood. Maya? Gone where?

The wind answers.

I look up the smooth pink incline of the largest
dune and see her running across its flank.
Arms flailing. Sari fluttering thin as a ribbon.
The sand stirs up behind her like a pursuing
ghost.

Akbar laughs. *Have you ever seen such a stupid*
girl?

I raise my arm but there's nothing left in the
muscle.

Instead, I catapult myself into the hill. Driving
my feet deep into the soft flesh of the dune.
But my fatigue upsets my balance. I fall

backward with every step. The harder I push, the more I slip. Soon Akbar is passing me. Muscular, light, his feet barely making a mark.

Let a man do it.

Maya disappears over the top. I make a guess that she'll turn left on the back side of the dune so I change directions. The crest is lower at that edge and if I'm right, I'll be able to get to her first.

Sandeep! Not that way! Akbar shouts. *The sand is too soft there!*

I pretend I can't hear.

And he's wrong, anyway. The sand is harder on this flank and I'm able to move quickly. Now I can see Maya below me. Thirty more steps and I'll be there.

Desert's hunger

My feet sink. The ankles. Calves.

I remember my father's warning:
The desert will swallow you if you're not careful.

Sandeep, don't move a muscle.

Leave me alone, Akbar!

The knees.

*Stay calm, Sandeep. Any movement will
cause you to sink more.*

Why do you suddenly care?

The thighs.

*Don't talk. Don't breathe. Do exactly what
I tell you. Spread your arms wide and then
lean back into the sand.*

*Why should I trust you? This is your big chance to
get rid of me!*

*Yeah, that's it, Sandeep. I want you dead. Then I
can finish the story about the Golden Child Who
Came in from the Desert and Died in the Desert!
Now stop being such an idiot and lean back!*

*All you want to do is put your slimy hands all over
Maya.*

*Oh, Sandeep. Your small, self-centered teenage
brain thinks that the only way for me to have Maya
is to get rid of you? Now you're really making me
laugh.*

Piss off, Akbar. I swing my arm into air and sink
lower.

*That's good, Sandeep. My plan's working. The
angrier you get, the more your body moves, and the
faster you sink! If Barindra wasn't coming down
that dune right now, I'd leave you here. Now quit
being such a little boy, and do as I say! Lean back!*

That's when we both see Maya.

She's running toward us. Not listening to
Akbar, who's warning her to stay back. I lift my
arms to wave her away and feel the sand suck
me down.

Don't move, Sandeep! Akbar shouts. But his
voice isn't angry. It's afraid.

Suddenly a sound wells up inside of me. I open
my throat and shout her name as if it's the only
word I know. *Maya! Maya! No!* But she doesn't
listen. She is running right for me.

Nightmare

I am falling. Down a narrow hole. Sinking into the darkness where air is thick and powdery. I reach up for something to grab, to stop the sickening descent. My hands open, close, fight for the sky above and then I touch it. The smooth thing. Softer than sand.

A rope thrown into my hands.

I grip as tightly as I can. Wrap it around my wrist. *Don't let go*, a voice calls from the circle of light above.

(Whatever you do, don't let go.)

Half drowned

I wake-up vomiting.

You should have let Akbar handle it,
Barindra says quietly.

You mean manhandle Maya.

I mean navigate the sand.

Where is she?

Gone.

I sit up so quickly my head explodes. Eyes
gored with needles. Light flashing white orange
green.

*Gone? What do you mean gone? Where? With
Akbar?*

*Maya did not go with Akbar, Sandeep. She ran off
after he pulled you out of the quicksand. You lost
consciousness and we were so concerned we
didn't even notice.*

Is he looking for her?

Yes.

I struggle to stand up. Head reeling with pain.
But Barindra puts a hand on my shoulder and
pushes me down.

No, Sandeep.

But the sun! It'll be dark soon!

Listen. It's possible that Akbar has already found
her and is on his way back.

It's also possible that Akbar will just take her
straight to his village and I'll never see her again!

Sandeep. Maya has chosen her fate. What will be
will be.

She has chosen nothing! You left her no option but
to run!

She could have told us who she is!

But she wasn't ready, Pita. Don't you see that?
Fear not only stole her voice but robbed her of the
will to help herself! And because of your
impatience you've condemned her to a life with
Akbar or death!

Sandeep. I am sorry. I didn't mean for any of this
to happen. I was just trying to put the safety of my
family first.

Then everything you've ever taught me about humanity has been false. You were supposed to see and protect her soul! Not sell it out!

You are young, Sandeep. One day you will understand the difficult choices adults must make.

A difficult choice? Or the soft weak nature of an ageing heart?

Alone

He returns in the dark.
No conquering hero.
No slave girl tied to his camel.
No Maya, safe and sound.
Barindra weeps.

See what you've done, Sandeep, Akbar sneers.
Maya's going to die out there. Is that what you
wanted?

You did this to her, Akbar! With your selfish lust
and medieval ideas about owning women!

I was doing her a favour. At least she'd have a
home with me. What were you offering? Nothing
but your doe eyes. She can't eat romance,
Sandeep.

And you only wanted her because you derived
pleasure from torturing me!

Well, you're half right. But I actually am quite
taken with the girl now. She's even more haunting
than the rumours. So, if I find her, I'm going to kill
two birds with one stone. Have a beautiful wife and
steal your future. Like you stole mine.

I haven't taken anything from you, Akbar!

No? The way I see it, you've robbed me of my life, Sandeep! Because you are selfish, spoiled, and think only of yourself! And soon, you will know what it's like to lose someone you love! And just like your dead family, the blame will rest with you!

Don't you ever shut up, Akbar? Leave the story of my life alone! It's mine!

You're wrong again, Sandeep. You see your history is also my history.

What are you going on about, Akbar? Barindra asks.

The truth, old man! About Sandeep's past! Where he's from! Who he is! And what he's done!

I don't know what you're talking about, Akbar. Sandeep's family died in a storm. No one survived to tell what happened. I know because I was there.

Well, so was I.

Darkness

You're making it up.

I'm not making it up, you stupid boy.

Explain what you know, Akbar, says Barindra.
Before Sandeep tries to attack you again.

On that day of the great storm it was my job to
watch over Sandeep. But he was a brat and he
never listened. Even then, people said he was a
bastard child.

Don't react yet, Sandeep! Akbar, you couldn't have
been there. Everyone was dead when Farooq,
Parvati, and I arrived. Everyone. Except Sandeep.

You're wrong. I wasn't dead. You just didn't look
hard enough. You didn't think that there might
have been other children?

Yes, we saw another child. But she didn't survive.
So where were you, Akbar?

My ears are ringing. Head banging as if my
brain is swinging inside a copper pot. There's a
question hovering, on the edges of a dream.
Another child? A girl?

I got tired of chasing after this little shit so I went in

Cathy Ostlere 329

a tent. When the storm hit I stayed inside. That's what I was taught to do. After that, I must have fallen asleep. When I woke the tent had collapsed under the weight of sand and I couldn't move. I heard people calling out. But I was too weak to make a sound. Days later, a cousin of Farooq's came to scavenge the camp and found me. Half dead.

You're lying, Akbar! I yell. Everything that comes out of your mouth is a fucking lie!

Sandeep! Barindra shouts at me. We will hear Akbar's story!

No, we won't hear Akbar's story because he's full of shit. Chunks of shit. Rivers of shit. Everything he says is shit. Brown, slimy, stringy bits of undigested palek paneer! Yes. That's what you're made of. Your own bullshit, Akbar! I'm surprised your teeth aren't brown. Oh, wait a minute, they are! Brown like your shit-brown eyes. Brown like your stupid camels. Bullshit. Bullshit. Bullshit. I don't know how you see, hear, or talk with all the bullshit that oozes out of your body. You're not my brother! You're a steaming pile of shit with a green turban balanced on top!

I never said I was your brother, Sandeep. You did.

The bitter truth

Well, now that everything's out in the open, I look forward to going home, says Akbar. To see my mother. Well, not my real mother, of course. I mean the woman I was forced to call my mother, or she'd beat me. She has an excellent salve for deep cuts.

I can't look at him.

By the way, Sandeep, I don't need your pity, says Akbar. If Maya, by some miracle, shows up, she'll be my consolation.

Barindra has to hold me down while Akbar laughs.

Shame

I don't know how you'll ever sleep again, Sandeep.
You've been the architect of Maya's fate from the
very beginning. Instead of trying to actually help
her, you've been acting like the tour guide for your
own infatuation.

Aren't you ashamed? She's gone. Your mother's
dead. Your father, too, who taught you that the
desert would reveal your heart. You quoted the
words but forgot the man! Oh, yes, and your sister.
My sister. Killed. By you.

The girl.

And you couldn't even bother to remember.

The girl in my dream.

December 4, 1984

Morning's light

Barindra goes south. Akbar west. I follow their
routes from the top of a dune. *Don't you touch
her!* I shout across the sand.

I watch my brother cross the desert, mounted
on his powerful camel. Bells ringing on the
bridle, green turban catching the first rays of
the sun. He looks like a warrior out of an
ancient tale. The evil one dressed in black.

I try not to think about what Akbar whispered to
me: If I find her, she's going to be grateful. Very
grateful indeed.

Maya! I shout into the air.

I wanted to search too. Take Moomal into the
north. But Barindra pleaded with me: *Maya may
find her way back. Stay. Wait. Please, Sandeep.*

Maya! I throw my voice to the wind.

He's afraid he'll lose me.

I wonder if Akbar is right?
Did I encourage Maya's silence
so she wouldn't speak and leave?
Did I keep her locked inside my dream?

KARMA

Maya the Beautiful. Maya the Lost Girl.
Maya Who Belonged to Me.

Did I want my story to be called: *Sandeep the Saviour?*

Maya! My throat fills with dawn and tears.

Waiting

For three hours. Five. Sun climbing to the
highest apex in the sky. Focusing its ion beam
like I'm an accused man in a dark room.

It's your fault, Sandeep, Akbar said. Yours.
Everyone left the safety of the camp to search. And
where were you? Playing hide and seek with the
goats? Don't you remember anything?

Last night I heard a breeze shake the tree.
Mother wore white bangles. They rattled when
she tickled me.

Do you know the worst part? Akbar said, while
packing up Mohindra. *Our parents called for you*
and our sister. They shouted your name. And hers.
But never mine.

I climb a second dune, but I can't see a thing.
The air is bleached white. Nothing exists
except a false wave of water along the horizon
line. Like my memories. A faint mirage.

No one ever looked for me, Sandeep. Not even
you. In your nightmares.

Barindra tried to make peace between us. *You*

are brothers, he said sternly. Your lives are
connected by God.

Not my God, said Akbar.

Akbar, did you ever consider that your mother may
have seen you go into the tent? And didn't call your
name because she wanted you to stay where you
were?

Akbar stared. A twenty-three-year-old man,
angry with ghosts for eleven years. Has he
been wrong all along about his story?

Sister

I asked Barindra where he found her.

Beside you.

Why wasn't I told?

He lowers his head. *I thought*
I was protecting you. From grief.

A word pulls at my heart.
There has been a hand inside my chest
tugging and tugging
for as long as I can remember.

Akbar? Will you tell me her name?

He looks down at me from Mohindra's great
back. *Malaya*, he answers.

Not Maya?

You couldn't say your "L's," Sandeep

Fire

I kick at the fire. Not quite dead.
The embers pulsing secretly
under cooling mounds of ash.

(Where are you?)

Barindra stirred the fire all night long.
For Maya, he said. His conscience
burning bright in the flames.

For Maya, driven alone into the desert.
For Maya, with no blanket for warmth.
For Maya, only a cold light of stars and
moon.

I push my foot into the ash. A flare bursts to
life. I throw some twigs at it. How high can it
be coaxed?

(How far?)

I try to remember what Mr. Banerjee taught us
about the distance to the horizon. On a clear
day, how far can one see? It depends on the
height of the person, he said. So the reverse
must be true. The object we seek must be tall.

(How far away have you run?)

I could build a fire on top of a dune! She could
see that! But carrying the wood up the shifting
slopes would take too long.

(Or do you hide? Nearby?)

The tree would burn for hours. And it's more
than triple Maya's height! She'd see it!

(And know it's me!)

I tug at Moomal to unbend her legs. Move her
to the other side of the camp. I don't secure
the moody camel, counting on laziness. Then
change my mind. She'll be afraid of the flames.

I scour the ground for branches, sticks,
desiccated plants. Anything dry.

I pile the detritus around the base of the tree.
Pour hot embers onto the nest and blow. Small
white swirls of smoke untwist, turn grey.
Tongues of orange flames seek the air in the
tangle of leaves above.

Then I fall to my knees and pray.
Amma always said: *There's no harm in asking for
something good to happen.*

(Now, Maya. Follow the light.)

The tree succumbs.
A hot pillar in the desert.
A beacon for the lost. To find her way.

My prayer

I walk into the desert heading north. I check
over my shoulder. I promise myself I'll turn
back when the fire's glow starts to fade.

Maya! I call.
Flinging her name into air.
Maya!
The name is a bead.
Maya!
In every prayer.
Maya!
In every hand.
Maya!
In every temple.

Maya is my mantra.

I call for her. To remember who she is.

Storm

The sound begins as cat feet
soft scratching
claw dragging
then a spit
a yowl
a hiss of sand.

I know this sound
this song of fury
how it grows
alive
into beast
with a soul
a rhythm.

The wind the wind the wind
it flies.

I face the storm.
The darkening air.
I test my will
against
a desert wall
the single soldier
of twenty thousand arms.
My voice is my sword.
Aimed at the belly of the wind.

Maya! I charge into the deafening roar
Where are you? I swing my blade
Come back! I lunge for the gritty apparition

But in the end
I am a coward
no hero
no warrior
not even a man
as I stumble
for safety
and a long suck of air.

Sandeep. The wind taunts. *Come back.*

Maya's tent

The canvas writhes like an injured animal.
A loosened rope snapping its whip.
Yet somehow the pegs have held.
And I slide inside, sheltering my yellow soul.

Tent flaps pulled tight against the wind.
Knot the ties. Twice. Then take a breath.

The air smells humid.
A stench of sweat.
And fear.
I smell my own cowardice.
And despair.

Sandeep.

Another breath. Lung tissue burns. Like acid on
flesh. But painless compared to the state of my
heart. The pierced muscle bleeds. With shame.

Sandeep.

It mocks me this storm!
Akbar's curse? My guilt?
The sleepless nights spent
calling for a dead sister?
But not a brother?
And now Maya too?

How many more will I lose to this desert?

Sandeep.

Leave me alone!

Fiva's Journal

Cathy Ostlere 347

December 5, 1984

Wake up

Why?

It's time.

For what?

To get moving.

But I like it here. I'm all alone. No one can hurt me if no one can find me. That's what Bapu said. Do you remember him?

You can't hide forever. If you stay here, the desert will take you.

Why?

Because that's what happens.

I'll sleep just a little more. The sand is nice and warm like a blanket.

You have to get up. There's something you must do.

What?

You know what.

But there's no point. I waited for him. Only death can break a father's promise. Bapu said that too.

He might have been wrong. So get up. You need to hurry. The desert is waking.

But why?

Because that's what it does.

Don't you think you're being a bit dramatic?

No.

And you're not going to drop this, are you?

No.

Fine. I'll get up. Which way should I go, Mata?

Follow the light, Maya.

My voice

I have a brand new diary!
A gift from Sandeep.

For your words, Maya, he said.
For everything you couldn't say.

His hands shook as he gave it to me.
My hands shook as I took it.

Oh, I have missed this.
A book.
A pen.
The empty page waiting.
Waiting for my voice!

The journal is delicate.
Hand-made paper.
Soft and uneven.
Mottled with dark threads.
Plants? Insect wings?
The spine is stitched with
unbleached string.

He gave me a fountain pen too!
No need to press hard
and raise the print through
to the other side.
The slitted nib will draw

words out easily.
Liquid thoughts.
Swelling letters.
A river of ink flowing
black and wet.
Flooding the paper banks.

Oh, I have missed this voice.
My written soul.

Thank you, Sandeep.

You're welcome, meri jaan.

My love.

A new life

So how to begin?
December 5, 1984.

Where?
On a train heading east.
Final destination: Delhi!

Now a salutation.
Dear Sandeep? Dear Mata? Dear Bapu?
Will I always have this problem?

I listen to the train skip across the desert.
Click. Click. Click.
The wheels roll over a scar of track.
Click. Click. Click.
Beating like a fleeing heart.
Click. Click. Click.

Dear Heart.

                                       (That should do it.)

Hurry! I want to shout at the engineer.
Hurry! There's something I have to do.

Click. Click. Click.

I must catch up to my life.

Dear Heart

I'm back.

Found

We found each other in the darkness.
Our eyes closed.
Stinging with sand and tears.

Sandeep. It's me. Maya.

No, it isn't.

Outside the wind screamed. Canvas pressing
onto our heads. Sand drifting between the
knotted ties like rising waves.

Yes, it's me. I followed the light. The fire.

No. No one could have survived that storm.

You did.

But not you, Maya.

Then who is next to you if it isn't me?

*The mind invents what the body desires. I've made
you out of my imagination.*

*Sandeep, listen. I didn't die in the storm. The fire
guided me back. You saved me. Open your eyes.
See for yourself.*

No.

Why are you being so stubborn?

*Because I can bear blindness but not
a world without you.*

*Okay. You keep your eyes closed and I'll
prove my existence in another way.*

I put my lips to his. I wasn't even sure how to
do it. Do you press hard? Soft? Is the mouth
open or closed? What happens with the teeth?

But it didn't matter.
We found each other in the darkness.
His mouth tasting of lemon and a cool river.
His tongue smooth like a sea-worn pebble.

I didn't know all sound could disappear with a kiss.

ℱlee

We're on the run.

Last night we raced across a purple desert.
Moomal galloping under Sandeep's whip.
A cloud of sand churned by desire.

See, she's not lazy. Sandeep laughs. *She just never had a purpose before.*

We run with the wind until the air clears of
dust. Stars flicker over our heads like far-off
street lamps. The sky is a compass, Bapu used
to say. Pointing the way to every corner of the
world.

A herd of red *chinkaras* crosses our path.
Hooves stirring the dry earth. Legs lifting in
perfect repeated unison.

See, Maya. One's never truly alone in the desert.

I don't think antelopes count as company!

Well, they should! He laughs. *Faster, Moomla!
Come on! We have a train to catch!*

He tightens his arms around me.

Hurry! I whisper into the darkness.

Words

I've missed the movement of my tongue.
The soft roll. Pushing the muscle between
my teeth. And lips. One's tongue is crucial.

I've missed the consonants the most.
An art of carving air into sound.

I whisper into Sandeep's ear.
My favourite sounds.
A word for every star above.

> *eggplant*
> *mountain*
> *mother*
> *tertiary*
> *bubble*
> *rumplestiltskin*
> *murmur*
> *ephemeral*
> *lunar*
> *matriculate*
> *mugwump*
> *soliloquy*
> *lunatic*

Your voice, Maya

Is running water for the thirsty.

I want you to know

Who I really am.

I slid my body from his embrace. Lips lingering
like magnets that must be pulled apart. The
sound of the storm returned with rage. The
silence broken with our parting.

It's time you knew the truth, Sandeep.

So much can be gleaned from two small books
hidden in a secret pocket in a backpack.

> (Blue covers stamped with a coat of arms.)

Amar Singh, Sandeep reads from the passport.
Lion. Your father is Sikh.

> (A lion and unicorn emblazoned in gold.)

Jiva Kaur, he reads from the second.
Princess. Lioness.

> (A British crown floats at the top.)

You're from Canada.

> (*Desiderantes meliorem patriam.*
> "Desiring a better country.")

You're lucky.

Happy birthday, Jiva

It's not my birthday, Sandeep!

It is for me. Jiva Kauer is born today.
And she is only fifteen. I thought you were older.

Fifteen and a half, actually.

I have a confession, Maya. Jiva.

What?

I searched in your backpack. While you were
sleeping in the attic. But I didn't find these
passports.

What would you have done if you had?

Honestly? I don't know. Can you tell me
something? Was Akbar right? Did I encourage
your silence to keep you near me? I'm sorry.

My silence was my own struggle, Sandeep.
Barindra was right. I had to choose to live.

I slip the passports into the backpack. A piece
of paper flutters to the ground. A butterfly. A
phone number written on the wings. And I
never want to call it.

I don't know if my father's still alive, Sandeep.

Then we'll go to Delhi and look. And if Amma's gods are on our side, we'll find Amar Singh and reunite him with his daughter. Maya or Jiva?

I like the sound of Maya on your lips.

Remembering

I've been writing since the train departed Barmer
for Jodhpur.

Words words words. Beloved words.
How did I stay alive without them?

My new pen is magic. It leaps through the images:

A first glimpse of Sandeep.

                                (skinny, big ears)

The narrow streets of Jaisalmer.

                        (twisted, the inside of a shell)

Mina.

                       (light-skinned and frightened)

Barindra.

                         (gentle as a prairie river)

Will you write about Akbar too? asks Sandeep.

Eventually. When the pounding stops.

When the pounding stops. Akbar's voice is still a
drum in my ear. A deep throb. Quickening like a
storm. *You'll be mine, Maya. Don't bother running.
I'll find you. I'll be the only one who can.*

Pursuit

Do you think they'll come after us?

Akbar tracking Moomal's footprints.
His stare reaching across the desert.

*Barindra won't. He'll believe that fate has
intervened. Though Amma will make his life
hell for losing me. And Akbar? How deep is his
vengeance?*

But *I* know that's not all of it. Some was my
fault. I had looked Akbar in the eye without
the restraint of a good Indian girl. I couldn't
help it. There was something familiar about
him.

Let's not worry about him, Maya.

And I know something else too: Akbar had the
voice of a snake that sounded like bells. He could
make a girl falter.

And he thought my gaze was desire.

Sandeep's story

He tells me what the desert unveiled.

An older brother.
A young sister.
A plea. *Say my name.*
His father's laughter A voice of bells.
Warning that the desert eats children
who run away.

White bangles rattle.
A child's voice whispers.
But no faces.
Except Akbar's.
The same eyes.

He cries with the truth that the desert unveiled.
His family.

What is hidden

Sandeep, may I borrow your knife?

The appearance of the silver blade wakes the
dozing passengers in the train. As if they've
been poked with the tip. A dozen eyes blink
while I slice open the bottom edge of my
backpack. The seam splits, the black hand-sewn
stitches, regularly spaced as railway tracks.

How many secret compartments do you have, Maya?

A mother on the opposite bench gathers two
small girls onto her lap. A shirtless man
wearing a woolen shawl leans forward as if to
hear my answer. His Brahman thread clings to
his chest with sweat. An old woman squints
and mutters a prayer to Lord Shiva.

My old diary falls to the wooden floor. Two
dozen eyes stare at the open pages.

*Life is an illusion, I read. And as it turns out, so is
death. What is real? What will remain when we
all fade away? Two things: Love. Forgiveness.*

I close the book and press it into Sandeep's chest.

Now you will know everything about me.

He holds the diary against his heart.
Dark eyes wet as ink.

*My family is in there, I whisper. And the burning
man. And my cut hair.*

For the first time since we found each other in
the tent, Sandeep says nothing. He fills the
silence with his weeping. He opens the book
to the last page. His finger tracing the words:

"A dream doesn't mean it's not real."

You must start at the beginning, Sandeep.

Four hours

Four hot sweaty hours to Jodhpur.

Sandeep turns the pages.

(Am I still the Maya of my diary?)

The train clicks over the track.
He doesn't speak.
The passengers go back to sleep.

Halfway through the book
his hand reaches up
and touches my hair.
I see two braids coiled on
the hotel room floor.
The sacrifice.
The exchange.

(For one's life.)

The symbol.

(Of grief.)

A part of our body
we can lop off
and not bleed.

Sandeep reads

He is meeting Mata, Bapu, Helen. My home.

Can he see the barn, the mice, the golden fields?

Can he imagine the sky? Blue as a bird's egg, a
vase, someone's eyes. Not eyes from here, but
someone's eyes. Maybe Helen's.

Can he feel the wind? See it bending the wheat
and the sunflower heads? It catches Mata's sari
from the window. Beckoning.

And Beethoven. The sonatas. Can he hear?

Can he hear my feet on the gravel running up the
lane? To the house, into music.

Can he smell the dark earth? Where I cling to the
dry roots. Hiding. Can he hear me hiding?
Breathing so softly?

Can he find me?

$\mathcal{M}$ute

What was it like? he whispers.
To be mute?

Like choking on tears
thick as a river.

How did it feel?

Like phantom hands
circling my throat
and squeezing
my sorrow.

Shhhh, the voice said.
Stay quiet.
Don't speak.
Not a sound.
It is dangerous to be seen and heard.
Remember. No one should know you are here.
Without a voice, you'll be safe.

I heard it all

What they said. What they were going
to do with me.

Stay away from my future wife, Sandeep.

After hearing Akbar's threat, I collapse inside the tent.
Stare up at the rippling canvas. Is it my body that
makes it shudder?

I imagine I'm somewhere else. Under a sky
streaked with white banners of clouds. A prairie
field half way around the world.

I am lying under the gnarled stalks of sunflowers.
The harvest is finished. Mata's music gone. Bapu
shouts at me, *Come out of there, Jiva! You can't hide
forever!*

Why not? Who will care if I disappear?

I hear Sandeep's voice: *Who gave you the right,
Pita? To give away this daughter who is not your
daughter?*

A bride.
A betrothal.
To a stranger.

My mother's wish too, Bapu said.
The promise of my body, bartered.
Or stolen.

My hands shake as if electrified.
Muscles moving by a separate will.
Is this what it is to be an Indian woman?
So powerless?

I hear my fate being argued. Barindra. Akbar.
Sandeep. Their frustration and desire beating the
air. Words like sticks across the canvas. Muffled
thuds, strike after strike.

Why not just speak? they all wonder. Or
write? My real name. My home. Why indeed?
Because I cannot admit the truth. The absolute
loss of the meaning of my life – my family. I am
alone. And wish to remain so. Forever.

I close my eyes. Urge the mind to go back to the
clouds. But they are thinning, lengthening into
plain white saris. The widow's dress.

I crawl out of the tent.

un

I run to the earth's curve
where the horizon is broken
by heat waves and clouds
where something is fluttering
in the yellow light
in the shattered yellow light
of a yellow mirage.

I throw my longing
against sand and sky
like a rope for a
drowning man.

Jiva! a voice calls.

I'm coming, Bapu.

Maya!

Wait for me.

Tears

Sandeep closes my diary.
Touches me.
A finger brushing across my cheek.

I'm sorry, Maya.
About your mother.
Your father.
About the Sikh man.
Even Helen.

His face is wet.
Mine too.
So many tears for those who are lost.

I hate to quote Akbar, but he was right about something:
When we tell our stories, the gods hear our sorrows.

December 6, 1984

Others

You're not like other boys, Sandeep.

                               Like my "brother," Akbar?

Well, yes. I mean, no. You're not
like him. And that's a good thing.

                                 You don't like tall?
                                 Carved cheekbones?
                    The way he growls and sings?

I was actually talking about the
boys in Canada.

                               You mean they're not
                          brown and funny-looking
                           with elephant ears?

Your ears stick out only a little,
Sandeep.

                               Ah, so you did notice.

I'm actually trying to pay you a
compliment. You see, the boys at
home are half asleep. Not at all
like you.

                               I am half asleep
                        riding this train. . . .

I mean they're dull. Or else loud
and stupid. And they smell bad or they
smell great and either way you want
to faint near them.

                          Ah! Like the Indian movie
                    star Anil Kapoor! Girls fall
                     down when they see him.

I was thinking more like zombies.

*You know, you talk a lot. Really a
lot for a boy. And you joke. And
you tease. And taunt. And argue
like a lawyer. And you honey-talk.*

*So true! Even now you
tease me.*

*When you speak English,
it's ridiculously proper.*

*You're serious.
Yet passionate.*

And passionate?

*Would you like to hear
me grunt in Hindi?*

*Not true, O
shaved head one!*

*Fine. How else am
I not a white boy?*

*Barindra insisted
on correctness.
E-nun-ci-ate.
E-ve-ry. Syl-la-ble.
A-ny-thing el-se?*

*I didn't use to be serious.
Not before you.*

*I didn't know what the
word really meant. Not
until you,* meri jaan.

A boy

I don't know how you wear this thing, Sandeep.

Twist this piece and fold it over here. Perfect!

But it looks like a giant diaper hanging between my knees!

You'll get used to the dhoti. Try not to walk funny.

The pale blue shirt belongs to him too. I slip my arms in and catch his scent. Spicy like black pepper. The sandals came from a man sleeping in a dark corner of the Jodhpur station.

Won't he be angry when he wakes?

I left him three rupees. He can get a new pair for that. He'll think the gods have blessed him with good fortune.

Sandeep trims my hair. The knife slicing close to my skull.

Are you sure you know what you're doing?

He left the front longer, hanging in my eyes, but the back almost bare. Now only stubble and a stubborn cowlick remain.

I run my hand over my scalp. Following the curve
of my skull. Baby hair tickling my palm.

Sandeep gently pulls my hand away. *Boys don't
touch their hair. Do this instead.* He shows me how
to flick my head to the side and throw my bangs
back. *Very manly.*

*You have no idea how lucky boys are not to have
pounds of hair weighing them down.*

Don't pout, he says. *Just flick.*

He takes my hand and we walk through the
station. It's a guilty pleasure to touch in public.
Between males it's considered normal in India.
Hand-holding, hugging, sitting on each other's
laps.

When I lean into him and whisper in his ear, *You're
wonderful,* no one notices. Except for
his blush. I laugh.

A prayer

Platform B for the Mandor Express. A crowded
second-class car. The seats are already piled with
bulky packages tied with string.

Sandeep approaches an old woman sitting next
to the window. Her spindly arms and legs stretch
across the bench. He smiles at her. She giggles.

He calls her Mother. He gestures to me. She
shakes her head. I hear the word *Mother* again,
and then finally she shifts down and allows
Sandeep and me to squeeze into the seats next
to the window.

*You promised to make an offering for her life and
health?*

*Yes. At the Chattarpur Mandir. A famous Hindu
temple in Delhi.*

And for that she gave up her seat next to the window?

*A blessing for a healthy life. We'll leave a donation. A
rupee or two.*

*Why doesn't she take her own rupee, make an
offering, and then keep her seat?*

Not as good as a stranger praying for you.

But why would she even believe you?

Because to lie about such a thing would bring very bad karma to me. And she knows I won't risk that.

So if a stranger promises to make an offering to a god, he is trusted. But if a stranger walks down the street with a turban on his head, he is assumed to be a traitor and must die. Is there no bad karma associated with that?

I don't know how murder is justified, Maya. Perhaps vengeance feels like the will of God.

I don't feel like laughing anymore.

Karma

Is there time to consider karma when a man is
running down a smoke-filled hallway, tearing at
a turban, scissors in hand, denying his faith?

Or when his body is lit on fire for a nation's
vengeance?

A turban.
A beard.
A *kirpan*.
Items to justify his murder.

Why don't murderers think of karma?

Fear

I look at the old woman. She has lost her place
by the window, but she is smiling. Her relatives
returned and were angry that she gave up the
seats. And still she smiles.

Sandeep whispers to her.
We are all afraid of dying in pain, or becoming poor,
or worse, being tossed on the street once a widow.
Should I make an offering to Shiva? Beneficent
Protector. Or to the goddess Durga for you?

Durga, she whispers back.

Shall I offer a garland of marigolds? My own
mother loves the scent.

She nods.

See how well life works when we work together?

(See how well we
trade on our fears.)

The old woman laughs. Pats his knee. Leans back
her head and closes her eyes. She thinks she got
the better deal.

Eight hours is too long without a window, Maya. You'll
see. You'll be more comfortable.

He did it for me.

(See how well we
trade on our passions.)

Discovered

The conductor in the dark uniform walks briskly
up the aisle. A man at his side is vibrating with anger.

Shit, Sandeep mutters. *Why couldn't this train leave
on time?*

Do you see? the angry man says. *It's a young girl and
a young boy. They were traveling together on the train
from Barmer. Unmarried. Disgusting. I wasn't going
to say anything, but now I must. They are on this train
too!*

I slink in my seat. Sandeep grips my hand and
stands up. The old woman slides into his space.

*See, see. Just a boy. And the girl is beside him.
The one without hair. She is a disgrace. She looks
like a widow.*

So this is how we'll be discovered! By a man
who feels entitled to his condemnation! The
passenger who rode shirtless, the Brahman with
the sacred thread. The mark of a superior caste.

*This cannot be tolerated. As the conductor of this train
you must do something!*

Sandeep faces the two men. The Brahman is

purple with fury. The conductor scratches at his miniature moustache. Checks his watch.

And then I see a woman coming up the aisle. A bird. Blue. Coloured like a peacock. She pushes past the conductor to get to Sandeep.

Brother! she laughs, gathering Sandeep into her arms. She reaches for me. *And little brother. I'm so glad you haven't left. Or I would have lost the chance to wish you well. Father called to say he thought you'd be transferring to Delhi. He wanted to make sure you hadn't missed the connection.*

There will be peace

You know these young people? the conductor asks.

Yes, Parvati answers. *I am Dr. Patel, and my two brothers are traveling to Delhi to visit our auntie and uncle. In Connaught Circle.*

It isn't true, sir, the man argues. *I have heard them talk. They are a boy and girl running away. Can you not see she is a girl?*

What do you know? Parvati says. *Are you a doctor too?* She lifts up her black bag as a symbol of her earned caste.

Will you arrest them or not? the man shouts. *For indecency.*

What do you care? asks the conductor. *Are they harming you other than your haughty Brahman morality?*

Without moral order there is no society!

Without compassion, there is no moral order! Parvati yells.

Enough! the conductor shouts. *There will be peace here. You, sir, find another car to spread your gossip*

in. You two, sit down, be quiet, offend no one. Yes, you do look like a girl, but who is to judge here and now? Not me. Now everyone, clear off. The train is about to leave. So if you don't have a ticket, Doctor, you must get off.

Parvati takes Sandeep's hands and lifts them to her lips. *You made a stone sing, brother.*

And then she hugs me, whispering, *You must be someone special to cause such a stir.*

Sandeep and I watch her float out the car to the platform. Her thick black braid is draped over her shoulder She raises a hand to wave. Golden bracelets. The sound of ice tinkling against glass.

I didn't get the chance

To tell her.

My real name, Jiva.
Born in Canada.

How my Hindu mother taught me to
believe that gods hear our pleas and
may answer our prayers, if they
choose.

How my Sikh father raised me to believe
that by living an honest and good life,
we are released from the birth and
death cycle.

That I believe kindness and
generosity is the karma we bring to
other's souls. Not only our own.

And that a boy named Sandeep
taught me. And his sister named
Parvati.

Thank you.

Gone

The night swallows our escape
and our voices. We dare not
speak and arouse suspicion.
Sandeep sleeps. Dreamless.
No cries of despair.
I keep watch.

The train travels in darkness.
A shadowy serpent.

It's too hot in the car.
Not even a breeze sweeps
through the open windows.
The passengers are uncomfortable.
Temperatures rise.
Flesh swells.
Voices murmur in sleep.
A single question seared to tongues.

It's true. You look like a girl, a voice whispers.
Who are you?

Too dark to be Canadian.
Too tall for a girl.
Too pretty for a boy.

I can speak three languages.
English. Hindi. Punjabi.

(And sometimes French.)
But who am I?
Always the foreigner.
Hiding in her skin.

Whispers in the dark

I know who you are.

Go back to sleep, Sandeep. We're not there yet.

You're the light, the jiva that fills the empty space.

Shhh, Sandeep.

Akbar had whispered in the dark too.

*You can tell me. I'll keep your secret. Tell me
what happened to your hair. Tell me your shame.
No? Well, maybe you've forgotten. But not to
worry. I won't hold it against you. You're one of us
now. A desert dweller. An exile.*

Where is the place?

I do not sleep while the
moon crosses the sky.
I am watching for the place.
Where another train stopped.
And waited.
White clouds spilling from the stack.
Unscheduled patience for the crimes to begin.

Will I know it?
Where the track curved?
The field and its stench?
Smell the certain death?
What my heart cannot bear
and cannot erase?

I listen to the wheels tapping the track.
Click. Click. Click.
A clock counting backward.
Click. Click.
Where?
Click.
Here?
Cli-ck.
Is this where the wolves came?

Hurry!

                      They are coming through the door.

Don't slow down!

Don't stop!

Gasoline on fear-chilled skin.

In the middle of nowhere.

A match leaps to life.

In the middle of nowhere!

Hair burning orange.

Not this field!

Eyebrows singed.

Not this field!

Eyelashes gone.

No!

The frozen tongue.

The silent scream.

His tears turn to steam.
Still in the eye.

December 7–8, 1984

New Delhi

The city is shrouded with amnesia.
A tattered veil of forgetfulness.

Four weeks ago
I left my mother's ashes
in a hotel room.
I left my hair coiled on a tiled floor.
I left my father in a city mad with hatredwhile the Indian
government looked the other way.
Citizen killed citizen in a fashion so organized it's
hard not to think the attack was planned for
months before.

Yet, four weeks later what is different? Fewer
turbans? But who is noticing?

On the streets of New Delhi, who is concerned?
Who even remembers?

I question the face of every man I walk by.
Was it you? Were you a part of this?
Did you take a man's life? His breath? His dreams?
Or did you stand by and do nothing?

The shame

I don't understand, Sandeep.
Where is the shame for what happened
on these streets?
Why is the city not on its knees?
The masses asking for forgiveness?
Crawling to temples with offerings in their
mouths?

Maya, we are a nation with a long
history and short memories. We are a
nation accustomed to pain.

Connaught Circle

Have you seen this man? Sandeep shouts into the street. *Anyone?* He waves my father's passport.

The crowd slides around him like he's a rock in a river.

We are looking for Amar Singh!

Women touch their jewelry. Hands press into prayer. The men shrink, but not all. Some stare at Sandeep as if to say, Who are you to ask? Why do you bring it up again? We've already forgotten, so do not come here and remind us what has passed. It's over. Forget. Like us.

Amar Singh is missing! His daughter is looking for him!

And there it is. A glimmer of something. Shifting eyes. The nervous ringing of hands.

Do you know him? I call.

The man runs for an alley. *I know nothing! No one knows anything! Now get away from me!*

His shouting brings a police officer pushing through the crowd.

*You are missing someone? asks the policeman. So
what? You think you're the only one? Let me see
that passport. Your Amar Singh is a foreigner now
so go to the consulate. Or go to the refugee
camps; maybe he's there. But go away and quit
stirring things up.*

Thanks, Sandeep says angrily. He grabs my arm
and starts to pull me down the street. *And on
behalf of all the murdered Sikhs, thanks for nothing!*

You bhenchod little shit . . .

And we're gone.

A plan

Sandeep holds my hands in his. To quiet
me. *Shhh. Try to stop shaking, Maya.*

I can't. I can't. I am too afraid.

Maya? Listen to me.
We'll make a plan.
That will make it easier.
A checklist.
You'll see. A plan will help.

Okay.
Sandeep's list:
    Rama Hotel
    Mr. Kiran Sharma
    Canadian consulate
    Refuge camp
    Hospitals
    Chandigarh

No! Not Chandigarh! Never!

It's okay, Maya. It's okay.
A kiss.
I will breathe for both of us.
A kiss.
Okay?

That *is* better.

Rama Hotel

- *What night?* asks the clerk.
- *November 1,* says Sandeep.
- *What night?*
- *November 1.*
- *We were closed for renovations.*
- *No, you weren't. It was the second night after the murder. The hotel was stormed by gangs.*
- *Oh, no. You are very mistaken. We had no gangs here. Next door, yes. The thugs almost burned the building to the ground. But not here. Not at the Rama Hotel. The staff would not allow it.*
- *You are a lying snake in the grass. Was it you who told them there were Sikhs in your hotel?*
- *Boy, do not accuse me of such things! Get out! Get out now!*
- *Not until you answer some questions. I want to know what happened to the things in room 12 G.*
- *No things. There were no things in any room.*
- *In 12 G there was an urn.*
- *A what?*
- *An urn of ashes.*
- *No! No! We have no urns.*
- *A man may have come back for it. Some days later.*
- *No! No! No man. No urn.*
- *Where's your manager?*
- *No manager. He has gone for the day.*
- *Then call and tell him that if I don't find out what*

happened to the urn in 12 G, I will tell every guest here that you've stolen a woman's ashes. And that her ghost is haunting the Rama Hotel.

- A ghost? No no no no. We want no ghost!
- Then tell me who came for the urn?
- Okay. Okay. A man came.
- Who?
- I do not know.
- A Sikh man?
- He looked Hindu to me. But I did not ask.
- Not his name?
- No.
- You gave the urn to a stranger?
- Oh, no, not me. I would never touch an urn of ashes. We had a cleaner give it to him.
- But he knew about the ashes?
- Yes. Yes. He knew about the urn. Who else would ask for such a thing if it wasn't his?
- Is this the man?
- I cannot tell from this photo. The man had no beard and had short hair.
- Did he say he had been a guest here? Did he ask about a girl?
- Yes, but I told him there was no girl. I had never seen the girl, so there was no girl.
- Did he leave a name, a number?
- No.
- And how do I know you're not lying? Or just too lazy to remember?
- Is that her?
- Yes. That's the girl. If you know something and do not tell, she will haunt you throughout eternity.
- On my own daughter's soul, I know nothing more.

Urn

Mata. Someone came for you.
You are not alone.

Kiran Sharma

There are seventy pages of *K. Sharma* in the Delhi phone book. One hundred listings for *Kiran Sharma*.

Start calling, Sandeep says.

> *- Hello. I am looking for Kiran Sharma.*
>> *- No. No Kiran Sharma here.*
> *- But the name in the phone book says . . .*
>> *- It is wrong.*
> *- Why would it be wrong?*
>> *- I do not know, but it is. Wrong.* Click.

> *- Hello. I want to speak to Kiran Sharma.*
>> *- Bad number.*
> *- But . . .*
>> *- No buts. Did you not hear me? The number you have is bad.* Click.

> *- Hello. Are you Kiran Sharma?*
>> *- Kiran Sharma? Maybe yes. Maybe no. Who wants to know?*
> *- I am looking for an Amar Singh. He has been missing since the riots.*
>> *- What riots?*
> *- The riots. After Mrs. Gandhi's death.*
>> *- I do not know what riots you are speaking of.*
> *- You don't know about the murders? The innocent Sikhs blamed for her death?*

- Rumour. Simply rumour. Not true at all. Now
go away. And stop spreading such lies. Click.

It's a problem, Sandeep says. *Indians don't like to talk*
if they can't see your face.

Then why bother having a listing in the phone book?

It's a source of pride to have a number. The real problem
is the telephone itself. One cannot see who is on
the other end. A banker wanting to call in a loan? A
policeman? A government official? A relative who
demands money? No, the phone is not for many Indians.
They do not trust what they cannot see.

We make over two hundred phone calls.
Only a few people are certain of their own name.
And none my father's.

Chandigarh

There's another number I could
dial. Written on the paper
butterfly wing.

> *(Just in case, Jiva, Bapu said. You*
> *never know when you might need it.)*

0142-3745900
J. Singh in Chandigarh.

But Bapu would know it's the last place
I'd go. To a family who can't wait
to meet me. And marry me off.

Are you done, Maya?

I show Sandeep the slip of paper.

Do you want to call, Maya?

No. They might lie and say he's there.

Ah, you're a real Indian now, Maya.

Why?

You don't trust anyone.

You're wrong, Sandeep. I trust you.

Heart

I take his hand as we walk.
Rest my head on his shoulder.
My disguise works well here.
The city cares for no one in particular.
Everyone has a crime or lie.
And we are no different.

I feel his strength pass into my body.

Every time I weep. Or get frustrated.
Or overwhelmed with the impossible
task of finding my father. He finds
something that lifts the heart.

A man performing a headstand in a small
green park. A flower stall heavy with
garlands of jasmine. The sour air from
garbage masked by the floral perfume. A
cow and her calf asleep in the middle of a
busy road. New born puppies rolling under
a newspaper. A jewelry store window
strung with golden chains.

Will these be the things I'll remember?
Not the fires? Not the stench of flesh? Nor the
turbans and scissors and hair? Will I remember the
smile of this boy and forget all else?

The High Commission of Canada

Closed.
One o'clock on Fridays.
Reopening Monday 10:00 a.m.

We should have come here first!
Now I have to wait three days!

                                        It is a very nice flag.
                                        What's it mean?

                                                The red flower.

What?

                                        That one. On the flag.

What flower?

It's a leaf. From a
sugar maple tree.

                                        So, this sugar tree is
                                        everywhere in Canada?

No.

                                                But it is red?

Only in autumn.

                                                And the red
                                                bars mean what?

I don't know. Nothing.

                                        Everything on a flag,
                                        Maya, means something.

Well, not this stupid flag, Sandeep!
The tree doesn't grow everywhere.
And the bars should be blue. For our
oceans.

Okay.

Sandeep?

Are you trying to make
me feel better?

And do you know how
much I appreciate it?

Is it okay if we don't talk
about the flag anymore?

He smiles but I see a
shadow cross his face.
A bird's wing overhead?
Or his sadness.
Three more days.
And then what?
What will happen? To us?

He's right. But if I look at
it too long, I'll just cry.

Maya, I know you're upset. But
the consulate will be open on Monday.

But I think the red works well.

What?

Of course.

Yes, I do.

Okay. I'm sorry. Three
more days, that's all.

I think it's the nicest
flag in the world.

Evening

Delhi is more desperate after sundown.

The homeless claim their square of shadow. Dogs
in packs dig in fermenting garbage while drunks piss
across their welted backs. Animal and human howl
at a moonless sky. In doorless doorways the
children limp. Boneless. Soft as putty.

Another night. Of dark-pressed despair.

Will the roads crack open?
Will the city that smells of bitter anguish
swallow her lost?

Don't look, Maya, Sandeep warns.

I will look.

I search the shadows.
Steal everything I see.
Dark eyes. Ragged hair.
Is that a nervous tick?
A finger touching a forehead?

I purloin every voice.
The deep laugh.
The word that might be my name.
I drag my memory.
For the details of Bapu.

$\mathcal{A}$ room

We need somewhere to sleep, Sandeep says.
Somewhere safe.

We pool our money. Parvati slipped us rupees
on the train, but we spent it on the telephone
calls. We sold Moomal in Barmer, but not for
much. She was so ragged by the time we
crossed the desert. Even her tears showed her
exhaustion. Or was it sorrow at being left
behind?

We can only afford one room, Maya. Will that be all
right?

I couldn't sleep if I was alone.

We walk back in the direction of the train station.
Where the cheap hotels shake next to the rails.

A really cheap hotel

A room for me and
my little brother.

                                     Your brother?

My brother.

                               Little brother is so tall.

What's it to you?

                             And silent. Doesn't talk?

He's mute.

                                          Why?

Why what?

                                Why is he mute?

Because some people ask
too many questions!

                             Thirty rupees, then. For
                         you and your little *brother.*

No, no! You're a thief!
I give you five and not
a paisa more.

                         You want a room or a toilet?
                              Thirty rupees. Or go away
                          and come back. Then it will
                                  be forty rupees.

I think your mother gave
birth to you in a sewer.

                                   Do I care?

Ten rupees.

                                  No. Twenty-five
                        rupees. Take it or leave it.

Okay. Ten rupees.
Three nights.

Are you deaf? Go away,
cockroach. You're wasting
my time.

Ten rupees, three nights,
and a prayer for your soul at
the altar of Krishna.

I don't want an insect
to pray for me.

No, not me, but my little brother
who has no tongue in this world
can speak to the gods directly.
He will pray for you. Tell me,
what ails you? Is it your eyes?
Your skin? Your heart?

It's my brain from
listening to you!

Thirty rupees for three nights. We
will be the most silent of all guests.
And you will have no headache.

Thirty and a prayer?

Don't think too much, sir; or
your brain will hurt. Just say yes.

Fine, you little asshole.
Thirty rupees. Pay me now.
Take the key and go.
Don't speak to me again.

Namaste, *good sir.*
You won't be sorry for this.

Oh, I'm already sorry.

A room with one bed

He sleeps like a baby
untroubled
by the noise of
rickshaws
motorcycles
and trucks
pounding the air
outside the window.

                                                (We don't touch.)

But my eyes stay open
with the sound of muscles
moving
hearts beating
shuddering
behind this cage
of narrow ribs.

                                                (We don't touch.)

He sighs in his sleep.
I sigh in my longing.
The bedsheets rustle.
I toss and turn.
Our breaths
filling the space
of a room
with only one bed.

I can sleep on the floor, Maya. Don't
worry. I'm Indian. I can sleep anywhere.

But not me. His flesh calls to mine.

(We don't touch.)

The refugee camp

You Hindu? asks the guard. *Wanting to cause trouble?*

No, sir, answers Sandeep. *As the poet Surdass said: Owing to ignorance of the rope, the rope appears to be a snake. I am looking for my uncle and my cousin here, his father. See, here is the man we seek.*

The passport is open to Bapu's picture. The guard barely takes a glance.

Go ahead, then. Don't expect too much. It's been a month and most have left. We had thirty thousand in the beginning.

Thirty thousand Sikhs? My promise to Sandeep to not speak didn't last long. *With nowhere to live?*

Where have they gone? Sandeep interrupts me.

Who knows? Maybe your people went back to the Punjab.

You mean, where we belong? I ask.

Well, isn't that what you want?

Sandeep throws me a look that says: *Don't say*

another thing.

Out of the guard's hearing, I say: *Isn't that the
thinking behind genocide? Religious groups should
either be contained or wiped out? And why are you
quoting Nanak?*

*He was a very wise man of peace. And he was born
a Hindu. Now please, Maya, try not to get riled up.
Just look for your father.*

Faces

Turbans expose the soul, Bapu said. They
make a face strong and open. Lift up the head
and shoulders. Raise the man to be tall. Like
the warrior in his heart.

But in here the men are small.
Terror has cut them at the knees.
Bending bodies and will.
Hair growing in hesitant patches.

Sandeep and I walk among the crude shelters.
The passport open to my father's photo. Heads
poke out of shadows. Lean into sunlight to get a
glimpse. The faces are blank. Even the children,
experts in dealing with fear, have emptied their
eyes of hope.

But they see something.
Through my skin.
My Sikh heart?
My Hindu blood?
Or my foreignness.
And isolation.
Such stares could burn a hole to the core.

No one in here has heard of Amar Singh.
And no one out there has heard of them.

How many husbands, fathers, brothers, and sons had
no welcome into death?
No mixing of bone and ash
with earth and water.
No cotton to wrap the body.
No songs to carry the breath away.
To the eternal silence.
Only the smell of gasoline — the pungent reminder.
Of humanity.

He isn't here

Don't give up, Maya. Keep looking.

He isn't here.

He might be under one of those canvases.
He might be sleeping.

Or maybe he's fallen into one of the latrines! Or
maybe the rats nibbled at him until he was gone!

Or maybe he's giving comfort to someone.

No, Sandeep. He isn't here. He's not one of these half
dead. And I cannot believe this is the best the
government could do for its people! This is their act of
compassion after failing to protect them? Where are
the cries for justice?

Maya . . .

It's a hell, Sandeep! Not a place of refuge!

Okay, we'll go. Just a few more minutes . . . .

I run through the shack maze.
Out the gate past the sleeping guard.
And straight into a naked sadhu covered in
turmeric paste.

Are we God's dream? he speaks into the
sky. His heavenly longing for mortal life?
Or are we are his terrible nightmare?

We are his crime! I shout at him.

Why do we dream and think we are alive?
Why do we sleep through the days of our
lives?

Because we cannot bear the suffering!

Ask what the human body is made of. Bone?
Flesh? No! It is the hardened clay of man's
hatred!

We are animals.

Sandeep's answer

I hear him arguing:

We are made of love. Love! Do you hear me, old man! We are made of the love that finds us. The love we make. And even the love we are fated to lose!

The sadhu's response

Ha ha ha ha ha ha ha ha ha ha ha
Ha ha ha ha ha ha ha ha ha ha ha
Ha ha ha ha ha ha ha ha ha ha ha

December 9, 1984

The wind

Creeps in from the west like a ghost.
Stirring a curtain of dust
broad as the horizon.
It blocks out the sun, its light and heat.
Sucks out the air.

I feel its breath whirl all around me.
Finding the corners of the room
rustling the white sheet
pulling at a corner
a shoulder revealed
in silent shudder
the sleeping hand
reaching down
tugging
for the cotton
but instead
brushes the skin
of the wind.

His name

Crawls up my throat.
Clawing.
Scratching.
Seeking the air.
I swallow hard
to clear a path.

Sandeep, I whisper.

The wind blows his name away.
Sand fills my mouth.
Shhh. You're mine.

Sandeep.

Shhh.
The desert wants to silence me.
Shhh.
Swallow my life.

Sandeep!

A flash of orange
pulses on the horizon
burning through the curtain of sand.

Sandeep. I'm coming.

To the light.

Remembering

I wake to him
leaning over me.
Head propped up on an arm.

Sandeep. You're still here.

> *Where else would I be?*

*Gone. I'm trouble.
Everyone says so.*

> *But beautiful trouble.
> A bad dream? You were
> crying out my name.*

*I was remembering what happened.
I was trying to
get to you. Through the storm.
To the light.*

> *You shouldn't have run, Maya.*

Into the desert?

> *Well, you shouldn't have run
> then either. But I meant from
> the refugee camp. You've
> twisted your ankle and it's
> doubled in size.*

And throbbing like a drum.

Ow.

> *Let me look at it again.*

> *You have a bad habit of
> running away, you know.*

I had my reasons.

*I know. Well, I think we should
blame the sadhu. I'm sure he
stuck his leg out on purpose
just to make a point.*

*Nice try, Sandeep. I practically
crippled the man and you're
trying to blame him.*

*Oh, I'm sure he was
already crippled.*

Now I feel better.

I gave him two rupees.

So little?

We can't afford more.

*I'm sorry, Sandeep.
I'm trouble.*

*It's okay, Maya. I'm exactly
where I want to be.*

We shouldn't be alone

Where are you going?

Why?

The bed is more comfortable.

But I want you here. Next to me.

Why not?

Not right? If love isn't right, what
is? The world seems more
concerned with acts of cruelty than
caring about what two teenagers in
Delhi do!

No, that's not it at all. I look
around and see nothing but hatred.

Then show me something different.

Back to the floor.

You know why.

Maya, the bed is better
in every way, but I'm still
going to sleep on the floor.

No.

We shouldn't be alone
in this room, let alone on
the bed. It's not right.

So, this is the way of North
American girls? You sit on beds
together and then you are right
away under the sheets?

Oh, Maya. Don't think that.

I can't.

*Why not? I think you've
had other girls.*

*Even if that were true, you are
not just another girl, Maya. I
am not talking anymore about
this.*

*You can't just not talk about things.
Give me a reason, Sandeep!*

Why are you?

Why are you so stubborn?

*Oh, fine, Maya! But you're
not going to like it.*

*I've gotten used to not liking
much of anything.*

*Okay. Here it is. I am not
going to take advantage of you
like my brother did.*

What are you talking about?

Why must you do this?

Tell me!

*I saw how he touched you
whenever he had the chance. I
saw the bruise on his face. Your
swollen lips. And then the time
you were only wearing a slip!*

*What? Where, Sandeep?
When?*

*I don't remember exactly! And
what does it matter? What
matters is that I saw you*

undressed and Akbar holding
your sari in his hand!

Oh.

You see? Your face is
gloomy and I just feel mad!

Sandeep?

What!

I don't remember that happening.

Convenient.

No, not convenient at all.
What if it's true?

Mute

Sandeep paces.
At the foot of the bed.

Three steps. Turn.
Three steps. Turn.
Three steps. Stop.

He looks at me.
Opens his mouth.
But says nothing.

I hear his chest beating.
The sound of antelope crossing a plain.
The retreat of the broken heart.

He's right.
The sari was off.
But I don't remember.
What came after.
Or before.

The door opens and closes.
A sharp click of the latch.
I have heard this sound before.
Men who walk through doorways
don't come back.

Memory

I remember Akbar grabbing me. Holding
me. I try to get away but his grip is too
strong.

He says I have to do something.
Something for him.
Okay, Maya? His mouth is next to my ear.
And I understand.

My heart is beating too fast.
Like the wings of a trapped bird.
But I can't refuse.
His voice sings.
And insists.
I can't refuse.

Maya! Don't! No!

I want to move toward this new voice, but I
am held back by the hands around my waist.
I open my mouth. A word, a name wants
to be said, but it's caught in my throat.

Akbar grabs the end of my sari and pulls.

Heart

The heart counts time in empty spaces.

One.
Two.

Eight.
Nine.

Seventeen.
Click.

Okay. I'm back, Maya.
And I'm sorry.

Twenty-one.

I don't know what to say.

Twenty-four.

I'm confused.

Twenty-seven.

No. I do know. I love you.

Thirty-one.

I love you, Maya.

Thirty-two.

And I'm not sure what I saw.

Thirty-six.

*Maybe it was all just a bad dream. You and Akbar.
But here's the thing. I am still not getting into that
bed with you.*

Forty-three.

*Because when we find your father, and we will, I
want to be able to look him in the eye and know
that he knows that I didn't touch you. And believe
me, he'll know. I will have your father's respect,
Maya.*

Fifty-five.

I will have my own.

Fifty-nine.

And I will have yours.

You can't hold your breath forever.
Sometimes you just have to breathe.

Sometimes

You just have to.
Not touch.

Flesh

My skin hurts.
Stretching
across the space
that grows
between our bodies.

We're not meant to be so far apart.

My flesh wants to go with him. Deep into the
city. Where he searches alone for my father.

Sandeep thinks Bapu may be at a Sikh temple.
Rakab Ganj in Chandni Chowk. Majnu Ka Tila
on the banks of the Yamuna. Bangla Sahib.

You won't be welcome in the holy
gurudwaras, Sandeep.

> *But Maya, I'm bringing*
> *good news. You.*

You're bringing tragedy.
Reminding them again of those
who haven't been found.

> *No, I'm bringing hope. Restitution.*
> *They'll see that.*

They'll see a Hindu.

Amends

I argued.
He's my father, not yours.

                                    And your ankle is the size of a balloon, Maya.

I can lean on you.

                                    You can barely walk.

We'll go slow.

                                    And what if we have to run? No, Maya. You'll have to stay here.

I didn't ask you come to Delhi with me so I could wait in a hotel room while you play the hero!

                                    I don't want to be a hero, Maya. I want to make amends.

What amends? You didn't do anything. And simply being part of a religious group doesn't infer guilt. Isn't that the whole point here?

                                    But who knows what I might have done? If I lived in Delhi, it could have been me wielding a stick. An accident of birthplace and I am caught up in the madness too.

You think the riots were about geography and religion? And not character?

And my character has not been tested! How can I be certain of my own courage and restraint?

Tell me, Sandeep. Is this about your sister? Your parents? Is this the guilt you need to amend for? You didn't make Akbar who he is today!

Sandeep shakes his head.
I don't know if he's agreeing.
Or denying.

Please let me do this, Maya. Please. Not out of guilt but compassion.

Okay, Sandeep. But know that if you don't return, I have lost everyone to this country.

Happy endings

He pulls me to him. His hand runs up the back of
my head. Then down my back. A thumb slipping
under the sari's edge. He kisses me until my fear
is washed away. But not my sadness.

Do you trust me, Maya?

Yes.

Then believe I'll return.

*You do realize that I've heard this
before?*

*There will be a happy
ending. You'll see.*

*There's no such thing, Sandeep.
When something ends, something is
always lost.*

*Maya, I'll be back.
By dawn's light.*

Future

He leaves with Bapu's passport.
A last look from the end of the hallway.
I memorize both faces.
A black-and-white passport photo.
Sandeep's uncertain smile.

How do you keep a man from his destiny?

My mother tried. *I will never enter your temple,*
Amar. What you call "a doorway through the
darkness of ignorance." So keep your belief but
not your community. And I will marry you.

Bapu hasn't set foot in a gurudwara in
seventeen years.

I'll wait for you, I told Sandeep.
But just till morning.

I have my own destiny to contend with.
In eighteen hours I plan to
limp through the doors
of the Canadian consulate.
If Sandeep's not beside me
I'll beg to be sent home alone.

The empty prairie.

What remains

I lie on the bed and take shallow breaths.
   In.
   Out.
Cross my arms next to my flat chest.
   In.
   Out.

There's so little left of me.

(Is that why Sandeep said no?)

From fingertip to fingertip I can
circle any point on my arm.
And my pelvis is like an empty bowl.
The hip bones hard, pushing through
cotton like two angry fists.

Would Bapu even recognize me?

I lie on the bed and wait.
Under the weight of the grey air.
Night smothers the city.
Holds its inhabitants down.
Skin to pavement. Asleep. Broken.

I listen for his movements.
Pushing along the Delhi streets.
Climbing the holy stairs of the temples.
   (I forgot to tell him to cover his head!)

I imagine I've given Sandeep my skin.
Wrapped him in my half-Sikh flesh.
Like an armor that will protect.
And save him.

And then I remember.
What happened.

The sari

Take it off, Maya.

Not for you, I want to say. But my voice is
trapped like a bite of apple in the throat.

Take off your sari. Now, Maya.

He doesn't shout. He isn't angry. But I can
feel his heart beating against my back.

Hurry, he whispers. *Hurry, Maya.*

I do what I'm told. Akbar's voice insists. And
I know he's right. He holds one end of the silk
and I turn, unwinding until the sari falls into his
hands.

Listen carefully. His voice is deep. Calm.
*You're to do exactly what I say. I'm going
to throw you Maya's sari.*

(Throw my sari?)

*And you're going to hold on to it tight.
Do you understand?*

(No.)

Sandeep! Say yes or no!

Now I understand.
Akbar's not talking to me.

Sandeep is sinking.
In quicksand.
Arms thrashing.
Panicking.
Maya!

(Say yes, Sandeep!)

Akbar unwinds his turban.
He ties the sari to one end.
Grab it! Akbar shouts.
Tie it around your wrist!

(Please say yes!)

He took off my sari.
To give his brother a rope.

December 10, 1984

Jiva!

I open the door to stop the frantic rapping.

Sandeep's face pours sweat. Damp hair hangs
over his left eye. Clings to his forehead.
Is it blood?

He cradles his left side. A broken rib too? But
he's smiling. His white teeth still intact.

He steps aside.

The hallway is lit by a tube-shaped moon
flickering and humming.

A man stands under.
A shrunken man with bowed shoulders.

> (Not tall like my father.)

The hair is cut short.

> (Not long like my father's used to be.)

A fresh scar runs down his cheek.
Thick. Deep.
A branch
a stick
a knife
dragged across
soft flesh.

The face is etched with pain and sorrow.

But the eyes.
The eyes.
Sunken.
Rimmed with shadows.

The eyes. Are on fire.

No

This is him?
This is the shell of my father?

Sandeep stands behind.
His hand on the man's back
as if he's holding him up.
He leans over.
His mouth near his ear
repeating the word
a name
I've almost forgotten.

Jiva. Jiva. This is Jiva, your daughter.

Then he straightens up.
He's so tall. Sandeep is so tall.
He must have grown since we first met.
Why didn't I see it before?

This is really her, Sandeep says. *Your Jiva.*
He gives the man a small push.

The man stands between us like a shield.

Sandeep watches my face.
This is Maya, his eyes say. *The girl I love.*
The girl you're going to take away from me.

No, I cry. The first word out.

Sandeep steps back. His eyes still talking.
What did you think was going to happen, Maya?

What did I think?
What did I think?
Not this! Never this!

I watch the tears pour down Sandeep's face.
A torrent of despair. A pain so sharp I fear his
eyes will cry blood.

I thought you would always be with me,
Sandeep.

THIS IS WHAT I THOUGHT.
This is what the foolish girl believed!
She didn't think she'd have to choose.

But we're too young, meri jaan.
We're just too young.

My love

He retreats into the hallway. Ducking under the
fluorescent lights. Backing his body into the
shadows of the green painted walls.

Don't go, Sandeep. Please!

The man steps forward.
Filling the doorframe.
Closing the space between us.

Please wait, I cry.
Wait just another moment, Bapu.

Because the boy I love is fading.
Falling down a tunnel.
Disappearing from my sight.
And my skin is on fire!

But my father cannot wait.
His heaving chest
the dampened cheeks
the familiar hands
quivering
reaching for me.

Wait.

His arms circle me.

Clutching like a drowning man.

Wait.

My arm wriggles free from his embrace.
Reaches into the sickly shadows.

Wait, Sandeep!

Bapu puts his hand on my head and pulls me into
his chest and all I can see is the white cotton shirt
and all I can smell is the sweat of fear and relief and
all I can feel is the pounding of two hearts. Breaking.

We have dreamed of this moment.
This unlikely reunion.
A father's tears falling
across his daughter's back.
A daughter weeping
into her father's chest.
This is love. It is true.
But it is not whole.
It is not enough, anymore.

When my father loosens his grip
Sandeep is gone.

My joy and my sorrow!
I have loved. And lost.

Let him go, Jiva. I'm here now.

Alive

Bapu holds my face in his hands.
He turns my head.
Looks at my hair.

God has brought us together, daughter.
Praise God. Praise God that you are alive.

God had nothing to do with it, Bapu.
It was Sandeep.

But God brought us the boy? Yes?
Perhaps that was his destiny.

No, Bapu. Perhaps he is ours.

Changes

We are not the same people any longer.

It's true, Jiva. We have no hair. He laughs nervously.
Grips my hands in his. *Perhaps we don't know each
other any more.*

This could be true. He's not the same frantic man
who left me alone in a hotel room six weeks ago.
He talks slowly now and only in Punjabi. Weighing
each word like a grocer.

*I didn't think I'd see you again. I prayed you were with
your mother.*

You prayed I was dead?

*I prayed you weren't suffering. A young girl with no one to
protect her. I know what they do to girls in India.*

But better dead than violated?

I'm your father, Jiva. Don't judge me too harshly.

He tells me his story

How he ran from the hotel. Staying in shadow.
Avoiding the gangs carrying car tires over their
heads. He hid in stalls and under tarps. He
followed the river and found other Sikhs. Ran
from them too. Unable to bear the sight of their
cowardice. And how they looked at him with
similar eyes.

They witnessed each other's terror. Condemned
the hastily shaved beards. Cropped hair. The
false denials of their god. They vomited on each
other's feet.

How had such warriors fallen to this place?

He hated himself. Even more than he hated
himself after Leela died. Self-revulsion was just
another weapon the Hindus used against them.

When he stumbled into Kiran's house the sun
was breaking the horizon. Slivers of light
splintered like shards of glass. The sky was red
and angry.

Kiran hid him in the shrine room behind a
bamboo curtain. Ganesh, the elephant god, kept
him company.

When Kiran went back into the city he learned that the Rama Hotel was attacked. But the girl named Jiva was nowhere to be found.

Amar practiced more self-loathing. He had abandoned his daughter to her fate. He had failed in all the ways men can.

He did not eat. Or bathe. He wandered the streets calling out *Jiva!* From sunup to sundown. Kiran walked with him. To the Canadian consulate. The British consulate. The French consulate. No one knew anything.

They went to the bus station. The train station. The airport. But he had no photograph, he realized too late. He went to the morgue. To the Hindu temples. He went to Chandigarh, where his family pleaded with him to stay. He even went to G. B. Road where the child prostitutes look down from the balconies.

He telephoned Elsinore. He spoke to my teachers. The principal. He talked to Helen too. Had Jiva called her? Helen cried. She asked if she could fly to Delhi. Bapu politely declined.

And then he stopped looking. And started praying.

He imagined the worst. Rape. Murder. His

daughter's body defiled, mutilated. Left to decay
with no proper funeral rites. The body not
washed nor wrapped in cotton. No hymns for
the sleeping soul.

His anger grew absolute.

Life

It's not easy to die, Bapu.

My father stands.
Palms pressed together.

Gori Sukhmani

*In the desert I thought I wanted death to find
me. But life is an enormous force. It doesn't
let go easily.*

Ik Onkar

*I've also learned that our lives are not just our
own. Everyone and everything is connected.
Like a wide net of fine thread.*

*Nam japat aagint aanaykay
Kinay Ram Nam Ik Aakhir*

*I don't think I know God any more, Bapu. But I
know something of humanity. The kindness of
strangers. Their cruelty too.*

Jis Nay Nam Tomarrow Khaha

*And I know the land's power. A sunrise.
Miraculous even though it happens every day.
The birds. Wild animals crossing the desert.
All of us witnessing the golden rays. Breathing
the same air. Does that sound primitive?*

Aagia Kari Keeni Maya

There was a man on the train, Bapu. They
burned him alive. And he cried for longer than
I could have imagined. It was his suffering that
taught me it's not easy to steal the will from a
life!

Ram Nam Jap Hirday Mahain

Are you even listening to me?

God will not

God will not let the murderers
get away with it, Jiva.

But he already has.

We shall see. *Sat Sri Akal.*
Victory belongs to God.

The scar

He runs his fingertips along the groove crossing
his cheek. His hand shakes. A new nervous
gesture to define him.

*It was a knife held by a teenager, Jiva. An angry young
man swept up in the moment. Swinging the blade this
way and that. Trying to frighten me. He held me
down with a foot on my chest and the silver in my
face. Where is your mercy? Where is your humanity?
I asked. He said he was keeping me for the others. I
dared him to finish me off. A quick push through the
heart would do it. But he was a coward. A boy afraid
of his manhood. He thought too much. And I told him
so.*

*Just do it, boy. Be done, I said. There are many more
Sikhs getting away as you waste time waiting for your
friends. Or is that why you wait? You want them to
see your courage? The murder of an innocent man?
You think there is strength in numbers? There is
cowardice in numbers too.*

*The boy waffled. His eyes shifting. When I started to
move, pushing at his foot, he became frightened.
Called for his friends louder and louder. Even though
he was the one holding the knife.*

What are you afraid of? I taunted. A shaved Sikh?

Unarmed? You're a coward.

That's when he swung his arm and missed. Except for my cheek. The ribbon of blood sent him running. He dropped the knife. This knife, Jiva. So now I have a scar. And a new kirpan. *Not ceremonial. The real thing. If a mere Hindu boy can carry it and wield such power, so can I. So I don't mind the scar anymore. It's who I am now. A hunted man. Beware the wounded victim you leave alive.*

irpan

You're frightening me, Bapu.
Put the knife down.

Hard

So. The boy, Jiva?
His voice becomes colder.
Edged like a blade.
How well do we know the boy?

What do I say? What does a
shared heart mean to a father?
Do I dare speak the truth?

I tell him how we met. Parvati. My silence.
The women in the alley. Bahrinda. Moomal.
The golden desert where Mata roused me.
Sandeep's brother and sister. His pain and
guilt.

And then I take a deep breath and explain
what it all means: *I have learned what love is.*

His answer:
You are not allowed to love whomever you please.

Why not? You did.

Proof

> Jiva, I didn't suffer so you could
> fall in love with a goatherd
> raised by Hindus!

And I didn't suffer to let others
control my life!

> You're my daughter! And
> you must do what I say!

I will not! I have proved that I am
more than just a daughter in this
world. What have you proved?
You abandoned me!

He gets up and walks toward the door.
He opens it, then slams it shut without leaving.

Well, you're stuck with me now.

The boy

The boy has
some instincts
and he might be brave
but he's reckless too
entering the temple without
covering his head
announcing to everyone
he was a Hindu making amends
and he was so smooth
in his fluent HIndustani
arrogant
naive
causing quite a scene
with his dramatic
shouting
pleading
crying out
Amar Singh!
over and over
and then
Jiva!
Leela!
Kiran!
the private details of our life
Elsinore!
Helen!
Neil Armstrong!
and finally

I'm in love with the girl called Maya!

The boy is a fool. He could have been killed.
I eventually stopped the men from beating him more.
But do not confuse this with compassion, Jiva.
You will not see him ever again.

I want to hurt him

Tell him things a father never wants to hear.
Recount the argument with Sandeep.

(Was it only yesterday?)

I'm not property. I'm not my father's honour.
And I am not his disgrace.

I know I shouldn't speak but I'm tired of silence.
I'm tired of lies. And I'm tired of hiding my heart.

This is my life, Bapu. And I didn't choose any of it.
Not your exile to Canada. Or Mata's suicide. Mrs.
Gandhi's murder. Or the terrible riots. I didn't
even choose to stop speaking. But I chose
Sandeep. I chose him to love. And I will not feel
guilty or ashamed.

I look at Bapu. His hands are trembling.
Searching the cleft of flesh on his face. Was
Sandeep right? Is it all too much? Is there nothing
good or pure left in the world for my father?

I'm not sorry for my feelings, Bapu. But you need
to know something. That foolish boy who risked his
life to find you didn't touch me. He refused what I
wanted to offer!

I feel my tears welling, but I stop them. They are

a weakness now. There are times for crying, and this isn't one of them. This isn't tragic. This isn't sad. This isn't about loss. This is about saying who I am.

December 11–15, 1984

Waiting

The reunion with my father is one of relief,
but little joy. We tell our sad stories. We
relive our fears. But we are angry and in pain.
Every subject is an argument.

You made a promise there would
be no arranged marriage!

> *I promised nothing of the sort!*

We refuse to see eye to eye.

> *After everything you've seen*
> *I thought you'd be proud of*
> *your Sikh heritage.*

You think I'm not proud?

> *Then how can you love a Hindu?*

We defend our new beliefs.

> *I won't make the same mistake I*
> *did with your mother.*

Which one?

> *Hindus and Sikhs should not be*
> *together. Nothing good can*
> *happen from such a union.*

You are wrong, Bapu.
I am good.

Sandeep

I am not allowed to say his name.
I am not allowed to leave the hotel room alone.
I am not allowed to stand by the window.
I am not allowed to use the phone.
But my father cannot stop me from imagining.

He will come.

Even if he has to look for me in all
the lonely places of the world. Cities. Deserts.
Prairie fields. School hallways.

He will find me.

And I will wait.
For his voice to call my name.

For Sandeep is like the wind.
No one will be able to stop him.

We are Sikh

The arguments are loudest in the morning.
We are refreshed. Ready to do battle again.

Khalistan will become a reality,
Jiva. God has seen our suffering
and will help us.

You said that would
never happen.

It will now. Sikh soldiers will
gather and be as one. So now is
the time for you to renounce your
Hindu blood.

That's crazy, Bapu.

I am not crazy!

Well, your thinking is! One can't wipe
away one's heritage with the sweep of
a hand. You wouldn't accept that for
yourself. You kept your hair long in
Canada. You wore the turban. So
you wouldn't disappear.

Your blood, Jiva, is the blood of
murderers. And since I am your
only parent, I will now say what
you are!

Or what? You'll bring out
your big knife?

Do not make me angrier!

There's more? Besides my heart,
and the memory of my mother's love,
what else will you burn with your hatred?

> Any Hindu that comes near you.

Is that what you told Sandeep? Is that
why he left and hasn't come back?

> I told him the truth, Jiva.

You threatened his life! Unwilling to
see his kindness and sacrifice as
separate from his family's religion!

> Jiva, I am grateful to God for bringing
> the boy to us. I recognize that through
> his actions, he has paid a penance
> for the crime of his people. But he is
> still a Hindu and cannot be in control
> of his emotions.

So, no Hindu can ever be trusted again?
Even those who helped the Sikhs during
the riots? Putting themselves in danger?

> No.

What about your oldest friend, Kiran.

> There can be no exceptions.

And me, of course.

> You must be cleansed of your nature, Jiva.
> But you are still a child. There is time.

I used to be a child. When I lived in
Elsinore. But now I am an old,
old woman. I have seen things no child
should see. I have seen adults make
a hell of this world.

Hell

I can't take much more.
My father's bitter anger.
My absence from Sandeep.
But what are my choices?
Run again? Where?
Refuse to talk until Bapu
comes to his senses?
Or go back to Canada with
a vengeful father?

Is this to be my future?
Like the unhappiness of my mother?
To love your family but hate your life?

What did you think was going to happen, Sandeep's
eyes had questioned.

I expected benevolence.
My father and I were spared.
We would be grateful for life.
We would choose peace.

I expected to be with you, Sandeep.

Pain

When Bapu returns from the
gurudwara he is even more fervent.
He grabs my hands. Holds them tight
between his.

So much suffering, Jiva. And for what?
So we can forget? Pretend it didn't
happen? Go on as before with
nothing changed?

You're hurting my hands, Bapu.

My anger is calling me to action!
I cannot stand by and do nothing.

What? What will you do?

Why must we Sikhs turn the other
cheek? Guru Gobind Singh Ji
quoted Shaikh Sadi, "It is right to
use force as a last resort when all
other peaceful means fail."

And have all other peaceful
means failed?

It is God who will tell us what do.
And then we will unleash the
Hindus' own Kali! The black
goddess of righteous battle! Her
coiled tongue on fire!

You are talking madness, Bapu!
Vengeance can't bring back the
dead. Vengeance is a hunger that

can never be satiated!

But the shame, Jiva. That's what we've been left with. Shame is an anger that dares not act.

A sign

I notice the first one on the top stair.
The blossom is crushed. A dozen pairs of feet
have dirtied the original colour.

The second one is on the bottom step. Kicked
against the riser. Already wilting.

A third one is outside the main doors of the
hotel. Still fresh. Perhaps fallen from a garland.

A fourth is on the pathway. A fifth on the main
road. A sixth is at the chai wallah's stall. A
seventh at the bus stop. An eighth, a ninth, a
street, an alley, then a dozen more strewn about
the temple courtyard.

No one else would notice them. The frilled
marigold heads. They're just part of the general
litter of Delhi. But I see them everywhere. A
carpet of deep orange laid out for my feet to walk on.

He knows where I go. Where I walk,
where I sleep, where I eat, and pray. He
knows every step I take without him.

He hasn't abandoned me! He hasn't forgotten!
Sandeep adorns me with his offering every day.

Sleep

Sleep is a good thing.
It separates my father and me.
We cannot bear any more
of each other's truths.

But even in sleep, anger doesn't
abandon him. His face twists. Emotions
throb under the scarred skin.

I have never been afraid of him before.
In spite of his height, his deep voice, his
belief in himself. But this small dark man
curled on the bed makes me shudder.

His faith, so gentle in his life in Elsinore, has grown
back ten times stronger. A hundred times
heavier. The enormous weight of duty pressing
down on his bones.

He sleeps with his knife.
Forgive me, God, he whispers.
For what? Are his sins still to come?

Will

I try to stay awake.

(He will find me.)

To hear the faint knock
that I pray I will come.
   tap tap
Soft, not waking Bapu.
I will slip into the hallway.
Into Sandeep's embrace.
His kiss.
His promise to return
fulfilled.
In the morning.
In the light.

But I sleep against my will
and don't hear the tapping
on the door of my dreams.

Falling

The dream-sky is perfect black. The moon in shadow like a
shy girl hiding behind her mother's skirt. Yet the
atmosphere hums. Then pulses with light. The pilot
strings the stars together with green ribbons.

Bapu sits beside me. But not quietly. His knees
shake. The yellow turban on his lap begins to unwind.
I pull at it looking for the end. *There is no end to faith,
Jiva,* he says. *It burns throughout eternity.*

I look out the window and see my mother standing
on the wing. She is washing the dark hair of the sky.
Mata's hands pour liquid stars over the silken strands.
When her comb catches on one, she says, *It's just a
snag. Nothing that can't be unknotted and made smooth.*

Is that true I wonder? I turn to ask Bapu, but the
words are blown out of my mouth by a great rush of air.

The plane is cut open to the sky. There are holes
where windows and doors used to be. Unbuckled
passengers sucked into cold air. And too much
wind to scream. As we fall.

I look to my father.
He will save us somehow.
But his face is still. Like a mask.
And then I understand:

the falling plane isn't an accident.
Bapu knew what would happen.

I shout at him:
Is this where your anger has brought us? Another
slaughter of the innocents?

His lips move but only a whisper.
I lean in so I can hear what he's saying:
Where is your mercy? Where is your humanity?

When the plane hits the water the ocean ignites.
I swim through the flames with the others. Our
arms burn like molten ore but our bodies are
freezing. We shout while we still can.

Help us! Save us from our misery!

Wake up

I wake in a sweat.
Mouth parched. Sucking for air.
I open my eyes too quick and I'm
blinded by a light.
I open them again but slowly this time.
Something is flashing in the darkness.
An object lit by the moon.
I know the shape but my brain
is slow to accept the truth.

It's a blade.
Pointing at my throat.

Wake up, Bapu, I whisper.

The knife turns, glints.

Wake up, Bapu. Please.

I hear his sharp breath when he realizes where
he is. He looks down at his hand. My face.
His eyes fill with horror.

Then he leaps from the bed. The bathroom
door slams.

He kicks at the walls like a trapped man.

The door

Someone is banging.
What's going on in there! Open up now!

I turn the lock. Open the door to the hallway.
Just a crack. Try to control my breathing.

Is he drunk? asks a man.

No . . . .

Then what?

The hallway is crowded with men. Crumpled shirts.
Faces creased with sleep. They try to peer past
me into the room.

There has been a death in the family, I explain. *We
are in mourning.*

The men nod and lower their eyes. They retreat
out of respect.

I am sorry, says the man. *But I am the manager and
I must inform you that you will pay for any damages.*

Yes, sir. Of course, sir.

If I hear another noise, I will be back. This is a

respectable hotel for respectable guests.

Yes, sir. That is why we came here.

I shut the door.
Fall to my knees.

I weep so hard I drown out my father's cries.

Goodness

Bapu?

I push the bathroom door open. He is sitting on the floor. The sink is pulled away from the wall. Shards of shattered mirror hang like icicles. The window is open. I hope the knife is lying in the alley below.

Bapu, I know what God wants you to do.

I do too, Jiva. He wants me to die before I hurt anyone else I love.

No, Bapu, that's not it. Do you remember what you taught me about Bhai Kanahya? The famous Sikh healer who carried water to every injured warrior on the battlefield? Even to his enemy?

I remember.

God wants you to be good, Bapu. Like Bhai Kanahya. He wants you to relieve suffering.

Bapu's tears

Oh, Jiva, things aren't so simple.

Why not? What's more
straightforward than kindness?

Before kindness there must be
forgiveness. For oneself. For our
sins and weaknesses.

What have you done, Bapu?

It's what I didn't do, Jiva. I didn't
fight to protect my Sikh brothers. I
didn't look hard enough for you.
And my inaction with your mother
killed her.

What do you mean?

I didn't say anything to anyone.
The trip was to be a surprise.
Leela would be so pleased with me.

Bapu! What are you taking about?

My surprise, Jiva! My surprise
for your mother! Two months
before she hung herself I
bought three airline tickets to
Delhi! I never told her she'd be
going home!

Oh, Bapu.

Don't you see, Jiva? I didn't
ease your mother's suffering
when I had the chance. I
waited. I waited! And for

what? For the selfish pleasure of her gratitude. You are a motherless child because of me. Where is the absolution for that?

KARMA

The dead

This is what they try to tell us:
Everything can be forgiven.
Everyone.

December 16, 1984

Sari

I dress in a new sari from the Sari Emporium.
Bapu said I could have any one I wanted. I chose
pale blue. A silk from Banaras. Blue is Mata's
favourite colour.

I gather the pleats at my waist. Drape the *pallu*
over my shoulder and turn to look in the mirror.
A silk river cascades down my back.

Do you want to know why a sari is so long, Maya?

I remember. The seamless fabric woven in one
long warp. Up to nine metres. But tell me again,
Mata.

To wrap a man and woman together on their
wedding night. Hiding them from the world.

I hear my mother sing:
Tall, short, skinny, fat,
rich or poor we fold and wrap.

Helen's voice, too:
Reincarnation. Another chance.
Everyone deserves a second chance,
don't you think?

Yes. Even Bapu thinks so.

Returning son of India

We walk slowly to the riverbank. The urn
wrapped in Mata's sari. My father's head is bowed.
His footsteps are slow like he's considering every
step.

Bapu's guilt has worn him down. And his anger too.
It's not in his nature to spill such hatred, such vitriol.
In some ways, that has cost him more than anything.

On Saturdays, I used to walk into Elsinore to watch
my father work. I'd hear the whispers. The ones he
had grown used to.

*It's the mechanic's daughter. Must be time for her weekly
oil treatment. How else do you get hair that black and
shiny?*

Ignore them, Bapu said. *Racism isn't always hatred.
Sometimes it's just confusion and fear. It's their own hearts
they're not sure about. Not ours.*

I learned to walk on like my father.
Wearing skin like an armor.
Carrying my shadow.

There were times I liked how my
skin kept me separate. No one could see in.
Not that anyone tried very hard. Except Helen.

*Your skin's like polished wood, Jiva. And your eyes
dark as obsidian. You're so lucky. No one else in a
hundred miles looks like you.*

It's funny. I don't fit here in India any better.

Postcard

I wrote to Helen yesterday. It took seven
drafts to find just the right words. Warm but
not pathetic. Inviting yet not desperate.
Intriguing, mysterious. Just a note to suggest I
miss her. Maybe we could become friends
again? I may never forget what she did but I
don't think it's right that we let a boy come
between us.

> *Dear Helen,*
> *I'll be home in two days. Before you*
> *even get this postcard! This is a picture of*
> *the Taj Mahal. If you can believe it, I never*
> *got to actually see it! There's lots to tell.*
> *Hope you'll want to hear it all. Oh, one*
> *more thing. I've cut my hair short. Will*
> *you really kill me?*
> *M-J*

Forgiveness

Bapu finally told me what he said to keep Sandeep
away: *Choose your heartbreak, boy. If I ever see you
near my daughter, I'll have you both killed.*

There are many things my father must ask
forgiveness for. He says it will take a lifetime to
make peace with his conscience. *How can someone
as sinful as me. Dare to hope for a place in heaven?*

In spite of waking up to a knife at my throat,
I want to trust that my father never meant what he
threatened. But Sandeep must have heard the
pledge of vengeance and believed him.

I can still see the grief in Sandeep's eyes as he
backed away down the hallway. He had done
what he promised. Brought me my angry father.
But the price was for us to be kept apart. The
space in between filled with cruel longing.

Missing

I looked for him. Every time I left the hotel with Bapu at my side. I followed the trail of marigolds. The crushed and beautiful.

But I never saw him. Like a desert fox.

I wrote to Sandeep every night. Tearing narrow strips of paper from my diary. Copying lines from poems. Begging him to show his face. I lied and said I was all right.

On the streets I dropped the crumpled notes like bits of garbage. Undetectable in the dirt. Unless someone was looking.

One afternoon I saw a child pick one up. She looked at it. She couldn't read but she understood it was something important. I put a finger to my lips and she smiled. She knew what a secret was.

I don't know if Sandeep found my words. And I guess it doesn't matter. The universe and a child know I love him. Maybe that's enough.

One last note

Live as a witness, O Friend!
The world is a magic show, a dream;
— Shri Bodharanya

At the river

Bapu holds the urn out in front of him. Shows it
to the rising sun. Kiran helps him take the top off.
His hand on my father's elbow. Holding up his
friend.

I watch how Bapu looks at Kiran. Is there
something in my father's eyes? A lack of trust?
I've worried that this friendship might become
collateral damage too.

But I'm wrong. Bapu kneels before him. He
places his palms on Kiran's naked feet. In India, this
is the profoundest gesture of respect. Kiran puts
out his hand and rests it on my father's head.

I follow Bapu's example and kneel before Kiran.
Without him, we wouldn't be here.

It was Kiran who returned to the
Rama Hotel and carried the urn out.
Nothing else was left in room 12 G.
No shoes.
No clothes.
The suitcases missing.
He never mentioned the hair.
The soft black rivers.

The urn was still on the bureau

where I forgot it.

For all the
hatred
anger
uncontrolled destruction
for all the
beatings
burnings
and unholy defilements
no one had touched the vessel.

No one had dared
spill the ashes of
a departed soul.

No one wanted such karma.

Ashes

My father pours the ashes into the Yamuna River.
They fly into the morning light.
Stars returning to heaven.

All things are on fire, my father sings.
The eye is on fire.
The heart is on fire.
And the body is on fire
when we return it to the earth.
For the sins of my soul, Leela,
I beg for your forgiveness.

Our daughter has asked me if love
is enough. Compared to what? To
no love at all? I think she wants to
know what happens when love is
gone. I will tell her
that love is always here. Carrying
us throughout eternity.

I kneel down and touch Mata's
sari to my father's feet.
I finally understand: *"To love each*
other is also to love the Divine."

Imagine

We stand wordlessly in the light.
Amar.
Kiran.
Me.
The first rays of dawn.
Bursting through the horizon.

I imagine Sandeep is close by too.
Like the man further down
the riverbank
lighting a ghee lamp
floating the leaf plate
for a soul.

I remember Mata's wish:
If I'm lucky, Maya, your wind
will carry me away one day.

Sometimes I imagine
it happened differently.

A bee
trapped between
the windowpanes
    taps taps taps.
Mata closes the piano
mid-sonata
listens to the house

quiet as a tomb
except for a bee wanting
to fly through glass.
She opens the window
the buzzing gone
but invites in the cold
autumn wind.
She wraps the *pallu*
over her shoulders
across her neck.
Just to get warm.

That's when she sees me coming up the lane.
Hurry, Maya! Hurry! I've missed you today!

I've missed you too, Mata.

Alone

After the ceremony, I walk alone along the
shoreline. Bapu trusts me to return within
the hour. I have promised.

I listen to the sound of India's voices for the
last time. Laughter ripples like water. A
prayer is a single note held long. There is
so much life here. And too much death

I feel a soft breeze caress my face and I look
up. An orange ribbon is floating through
the air. In India, it's easy to see the wind.

Maya!

I look around.

Maya!

A tall man emerges from the water like a
charging buffalo.

I have something for you!

He holds a brown-paper package above his head.
His mouth is grinning.
His ears stick out just a little too much.

I watch him approach. White shirt clinging to his chest. A garland circling his neck like groom's. Marigolds!

My hands reach for him without thinking.

A chance

When he steps out of the muddy shallows,
I fight the desire to fall into his arms.
For I am dressed as a girl now.

I watch Sandeep flick his head back. The
hair throws tiny prisms of water across my
shouders. I want to laugh but I must show
all decorum in this public place.

*You're soaked, Sandeep! Don't you think it's a
bit cold to sip in these waters?*

*I wanted to cleanse my soul before I saw you,
Maya.*

You knew I'd be alone?

*I didn't. But I've been watching, waiting for the
chance. And suddenly it was here. And I took
it.*

Marigolds

He lifts the necklace of orange blossoms
and lowers it over my head. These are for
you. *Sorry, they're a bit wet.*

Oh, I don't mind. I can't stop smiling!

*I have something else for you. A gift to take
home. He puts the brown-paper package
into my hands. It's my journal.*

Oh, Sandeep. Are you sure?

*I am. I want you to have it. It was always
intended for you.*

But it's your story, Sandeep. Your life.

And I offer it to you, if you want it.

I take the book into my hands and cannot
speak. Within these pages is the story of my
silence. And my terrible fear. And my love.

*And one more thing, Maya? Don't cheat and
read the last page first.*

I laugh. It's good to laugh with your best
friend. Especially while you're crying.

The future

I'm leaving tonight, Sandeep.

Oh. Well, part of me is glad.

Why?

Because now I know Amar isn't marrying you off to a widower with five bratty children.

You're right. That is good news.

Are you looking forward to going home? Getting out of this crazy country?

Looking forward to leaving you? No. A thousand no's. But I can't stay. And you can't come.

Not yet, Maya. But we're young. Our futures aren't set yet. Anything can happen. I could finish high school. Wouldn't Amma be pleased? I may even go to university. Become a doctor like Parvati. Does Canada need doctors?

It will take ten years, Sandeep!

And by then will you be too old and ugly to marry? Or just too smart?

How will I live without him?

My gift

I take Mata's sari from around my shoulders.

I have a present for you too, Sandeep.

I hold one end and give him the other. We
fold it in half. Eyes meeting, unblinking. Then
half again. Fingers touching. Our bodies step
closer and closer with each new fold. When
we are done we hold a perfect square of
orange between us.

I place the sari in Sandeep's hands.
He bows deeply to me. His tears
falling onto the silk.

I know we're not supposed to touch
but my hand reaches for him. Across
the space between us. The sorrow in
my skin lifting and carried away by the wind.

Her skin smells like mint, he whispers.
*Her mouth tastes like lemon
and a cool river.
Her tongue is round like
a pebble in my mouth.
She quenches all of my thirsts.*

I touch his forehead with my palm.

I live here, Sandeep. Forever.

And here too, he says. He kisses my
fingers and holds them to his lips.

Not yet

It is the moment to say goodbye. But we stand. Not moving. Unable to part. Tears stain our cheeks.

What will you do? After today?

I was thinking of going to look for Akbar.

He's going to be furious that we sold Moomal.

He's pretty furious about a lot of things. But he's my brother. And he did save my life.

You remembered.

Yes. I worked it out. I remembered why he was holding your sari. Please forgive me, Maya.

It was a day we both wanted to forget, Sandeep. And we did.

Do you think there's more? More that we've forgotten?

There's only one other thing I wish I could remember. But it never happened.

We both know what I'm talking about. The

moment in the hotel when he stopped me
from undressing.

We kiss on the river's edge but keep our
hands at our sides. There's no sense in
calling more attention than necessary.
We've learned restraint.

December 17, 1984

Home

As the plane lifts off the ground I look
over at my father. His eyes are closed.
His legs stretched out. He has no
paper-wrapped carry-on for this flight.

He wears his turban. The long length of
navy cotton that I watched him twist
and fold in an act of focused meditation.
I have a feeling it will remain on his head
for the long trip home.

Will you write to me? I asked Sandeep before
we parted.

If your father allows it.

*It'll be all right. Bapu's faith requires him to
seek forgiveness for his sins. And he believes
he has wronged you.*

*Then I shall write. And promise to find you,
again,* meri jaan. *Here. There.
Somewhere in between here and there.*

I lean down and pull out Sandeep's gift
from under the seat in front of me.
Untie the string and remove the thick
waxy wrapping.

On top of the notebook is a small piece of paper.
A hand has smoothed out the wrinkles.
The words are barely legible.
Smeared from the oblivious
crush of a thousand Indian feet.
But I know what they say.
I wrote them:

> *We cannot see how our lives will unfold.*
> *What is destiny and what is accident?*
> *And how can one ever be certain?*
> *— M.*

Last page

I can't stop myself.
I open the notebook from the back.
Flip the pages until I find Sandeep's final entry.

December 4, 1984
(written on December 15)

Akbar! I call to him. *One more thing I
need to know.*

What? He pulls on Mohindra's powerful
neck. Turns the animal so he can face
me.

Tell me my real name.

See? You are curious like me.

The name?

*Little brother, on the night you were born
our mother had a dream about Mohammad
going to the Seventh Heaven. She called
you Miraj after the Prophet's great journey.*

And is Akbar your real name?

Maybe yes. Maybe no. Perhaps one day

you will know the truth. When your memory rises out of the desert like a buried city.

But if it does, Akbar? I don't expect to live there.

Of course you don't. But remember that you and I are more alike than you know.

Longing

Miraj.

I close my eyes and imagine he's with me. Holding
my face in slender hands. Lips soft and dark—a
cinnamon bloom. A poet's words fall from his
mouth into mine: I desire my beloved only / And
there is no other wish in my heart. I touch the
memory of his arm. From wrist to shoulder.
Coffee skin. Thin and close to the bone.

My lover's name is Miraj.

We find each other in the darkness. Our longing is
our guide out of innocence. Tongues too. We are
awkward but tender in our shyness. Do we
hesitate? Hold back? Perhaps only to take a
breath. For our desire is like a sea. Wave upon
wave. Until our souls lay bare and exposed upon a
far-off shore and our grief is eased.

The young are told to wait for emotions to catch
up to the flesh but what if the moment is now?
Our yearnings ready to set us free from sorrow
and fear?

And besides, who will show the world the
possibility of love, if it isn't us?

The End

Many many thanks

for support
Alberta Foundation for the Arts
Canada Council for the Arts

for strength
Rand

for joy
Victoria, David, Tegan, Leda, Mark

for reading
Charlotte Gill
Sue Hill
Victor Ramraj
Paulina Redfern

for guidance
Nadeem Parmar

for wisdom
John Pearce

for enthusiasm
Caitlin Drake
Jennifer Notman

for vision
Razorbill/Penguin Group (USA)
Puffin Canada/Penguin Group (Canada)

for stewardship
Gillian Levinson

for believing
Jessica Rothenberg

for inspiration
the people of India